'Is your mother visiting someone?'

The fluorescent light flickered and then he was staring at her across the room.

'Uh-oh! Not so young after all.' The attractive voice was now soft and husky. Sexy, came the unbidden thought. His gaze was appreciatively lingering on her delicate curves. Then he raised his eyes slowly to examine her face. Their eyes locked.

Suddenly he grinned at her, his whole face lighting up with mischief and masculine appreciation.

Dear Reader

August is for holidays and the four books this month should beguile your time. Caroline Anderson offers ROLE PLAY, where GP Leo hides his emotions; family difficulties abound in Lilian Darcy's CONFLICTING LOYALTIES alongside an insight to a burns unit; ONGOING CARE by Mary Hawkins continues the theme raised in PRIORITY CARE and updates those people; and, in A DEDICATED VET by Carol Wood, Gina has a lot to prove about herself. All good stuff!

The Editor

!!!STOP PRESS!!! If you enjoy reading these medical books, have you ever thought of writing one? We are always looking for new writers for LOVE ON CALL, and want to hear from you. Send for the guidelines, with SAE, and start writing!

Mary Hawkins lives with her minister husband and two of their three grown children in the Hunter Valley north of Sydney, but still thinks of herself as a Queenslander! She is a registered nurse who returned to her profession several years ago after a long break and found tremendous changes in the medical world. Now her love of nursing has been surpassed by her love of writing, but close contacts in the medical profession help keep her stories current and real to life.

Recent titles by the same author:

PRIORITY CARE

ONGOING CARE

BY

MARY HAWKINS

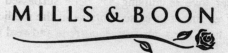

MILLS & BOON LIMITED
ETON HOUSE, 18-24 PARADISE ROAD
RICHMOND, SURREY TW9 1SR

MILLS & BOON, the Rose Device and LOVE ON CALL
are trademarks of the publisher.

First published in Great Britain 1994
by Mills & Boon Limited

© Mary Hawkins 1994

Australian copyright 1994 Philippine copyright 1994
This edition 1994

ISBN 0 263 78733 8

Set in Times 10 on 11 pt.

03-9408-45883

Made and printed in Great Britain

CHAPTER ONE

ELLENA closed her eyes for a moment and raised her hand to massage the sharp pain at the back of her head. She sighed, acknowledging how stupid she had been coming to her office first instead of going straight to her flat.

Trying to ignore the now persistent headache, she bent over to pick up the last African violet in her grandmother's favourite china plant-pot.

'Now, I wonder where on earth you've come from, young lady?'

The strong masculine voice behind her held more than a trace of exasperation.

Ellena froze and closed her eyes. The last thing she needed tonight was to meet one of the staff. She'd hoped the nurses would all be busy settling the patients in their rooms for the night, and the office staff would have gone home ages ago. But this voice was unfamiliar and he obviously didn't know who she was. They had needed more nursing staff even before her own unexpected leave of six weeks. No doubt Julie had gone ahead and appointed——

'*And* I also wonder how on earth you got into this office! She must have left the door unlocked again.' The voice sounded sharp with authority, but rather fed up.

Ellena straightened slowly, both hands holding the African violet. She frowned. It wasn't like Julie to neglect something so basic as locking up properly.

5

She heard him move, and swung around just as the deep baritone said firmly, 'Look, you've no business being in here. Especially in here.' He paused briefly as she faced him.

Ellena had only turned on the desk lamp, hoping no one would notice the light on in the DON's office and investigate. Now she was even more glad of the dim light as he peered at her.

'This is the dragon lady's office, and she'll be back next week. Is your mother visiting someone? Visiting hours are over now, and you should be gone.'

Twenty-nine-year-old director of nursing at the Macallister Geriatric Rehabilitation Complex, Ellena Irene Provis, suddenly realised that this stranger thought she was just a girl!

Many times in the past, her slight build and one-hundred-and-fifty-centimetre height had been responsible for her age and maturity being mistaken for that of someone much younger. It had always annoyed her immensely. But that mistake had not happened for years now.

She scowled as she pushed back a few loose strands of long blonde hair behind her ears, wishing it were pinned up in its usual thick knob on the top of her head instead of the long single plait fastened with a rubber band. She'd always somehow felt that the thick roll added the extra inches she needed, the extra confidence she needed to. . .to deal with. . .

Suddenly she stilled.

'Whose office did you say this was?'

Even to her own ears her voice sounded far too loud, far too aggressive.

The man moved suddenly and reached out to the switch near the open door. The fluorescent light flickered and then he was staring at her across the room.

'Uh-oh! Not so young after all,' Ellena heard him mutter.

As she thankfully noted he wasn't wearing a staff uniform, her eyes flickered up to his face. Suddenly the angry words that had been about to burst out died on her lips. He was the most striking-looking man she had ever seen.

Black eyes set in long eyelashes under black eyebrows captured hers. One of the thickest black moustaches she had ever seen dominated a pair of beautifully shaped lips. He moved slightly and a wayward curl from the mop of thick black wavy hair fell on to his wide, darkly tanned forehead.

He doesn't need that moustache, she thought a little wildly; his face is much too strong as it is!

Her eyes moved lower. Although he was much taller than her he still would have been only average height, but was very powerfully built. That dark suit and pale blue shirt couldn't disguise the fact he was very well put together!

A tie must have been carelessly discarded as the white collar was only partly turned down. A thick, curling mass of black hair was on view where the shirt had been undone. Her eyes started to drift lower and then she realised she was examining him as she never had another man before. Horrified, her glance flashed back to his face, only to find those incredible eyes were sweeping slowly down her own body. She saw one thick dark eyebrow quirk upwards, and ridiculously her heart sank as she realised what a wreck she presented.

When she had looked in the mirror briefly that

morning she had noted the black circles around
red-streaked eyes set in a pale face. Then today had
been even more dreadful than before, and that last
two hours of travelling from Scone, up the Hunter
River Valley, had been the last straw. She was
thoroughly exhausted. Her jeans and T-shirt were
filthy from that final bout of clearing out the old, neglected farmhouse and cramming everything she could
of her carefully selected memories into her car.

But it had been one of her last promises to Gran
that she would keep her carefully nurtured African
violets in just the right spot to catch the morning sun.
She had not been able to think of anywhere suitable
in her one-bedroom flat. They could have stayed
packed in the box one more night, but it would have
meant another trip here tomorrow when staff would
be around, and the way home had meant driving right
past Macallister's. Well, at least, that was how she had
justified her sudden impulse.

Deep down, she knew that it was as much to delay
going back to those tiny, lonely rooms. This office was
the centre of her new life. Another step up in the
career she had pursued with such enthusiasm and
commitment.

'Uh-oh! Very definitely older!'

The attractive voice was now soft and husky. Sexy,
came the unbidden thought.

His gaze was once again appreciatively lingering on
her delicate curves. Then he raised his eyes slowly to
examine her face. Their eyes locked.

Suddenly he grinned at her, his whole face lighting
up suddenly with mischief and masculine appreciation.

She stiffened. Her chin came up. Something about
the admiring gleam in those eyes made her catch her

breath. As she slowly released the air in her lungs she suddenly felt apprehensive.

Whoever this man was, she did not like him. He was much too handsome, much too everything for his own good!

And for any poor susceptible woman, a little wayward inner voice added.

Besides, she reminded herself hurriedly, she had always hated a moustache on a man. And she simply loathed the way this particular one had twitched quite ridiculously when he smiled.

She opened her mouth to order him out of her office, and then paused. Her dirty and untidy appearance put her at a distinct disadvantage, and every instinct was warning her that she would need to be very careful around this man if he worked here too.

'What are you doing with that pot-plant?'

His voice was full of amusement, and she glanced down helplessly at the plant in her hand.

What was she doing with it?

Pain jabbed even more viciously in her head and sudden tears flooded her tired eyes as a wave of sadness and loneliness swept through her.

She turned her back on him and placed it beside the rest of the plants on the wide windowsill.

'Good heavens!' she heard him exclaim. 'There must be a dozen of them!'

This one had an abundance of pure white flowers nestled among the green velvet leaves. She fussed with a couple of the other pots, repositioning one with deep pink blossoms so that the flowers would be more visible from the office, while she tried to hurriedly blink away the moisture in her eyes.

How could she explain the need she had to bring

something so dear to her beloved grandmother into her place of work, where she could look after them, see them every day?

'Are you a friend of Sister Terry? Was the door left open for you to deliver them?'

Who on earth was Sister Terry?

Ellena swallowed rapidly, and after a moment said quickly, 'Yes, something like that. I've finished now.'

To her dismay, her voice sounded very husky. Without looking at him, she picked up the empty box and started forward, fearing that sheer exhaustion would cause her to dissolve into a very uncharacteristic flood of tears.

He hadn't moved from his position in front of the door, and she was forced to stop a couple of paces away and look at him. He was examining the colourful row of plants with a frown. One hand came up and a finger and thumb smoothed down the moustache.

'They look very nice, but I'm not certain it's a good idea. Do you think Miss Provis will mind these cluttering up her windowsill like that? And you've pulled the curtains right back, too,' he accused with a snap in his voice as he swung his glance to her face.

Once again she found herself tilting her chin defensively at him.

'I'm sure she won't mind,' she said as firmly as she could. 'They. . .they'll be very useful for. . .for diversional therapy for. . .for the patients,' she heard herself add a shade too rapidly, trying to stop the telltale tremble in her voice.

The expression on his face changed. He straightened, and his gaze pierced through her. A question flashed into his eyes as she held his look for a brief moment.

She looked quickly away and nodded towards the door. 'If you would excuse me?'

She cleared her throat. Confound it. She must be even more tired than she'd thought. Her voice had positively squeaked out then, not at all like her usually confident, authoritative tones.

He didn't move, his glance once again rapidly sweeping over the untidy clothes and settling on her hair before returning to study her eyes. Something about the breadth of his shoulders, the set of the strong jaw and that. . .that look in his eyes made him suddenly appear rather intimidating.

Indignation, even a hint of anger tinged with some trepidation, began to stir somewhere deep inside her.

'Would you move out of my way? Right now, please!'

This time her voice had come out strongly, a little too loudly.

'You're upset,' he said slowly. 'I'm sorry. I didn't mean to sound so annoyed.'

Once again, lean brown fingers smoothed down the moustache. He gave a deep sigh and something deep inside Ellena responded. She felt a momentary confusion as he smiled slightly again, deep laughter lines deepening each side of that ridiculous moustache. An odd feeling of relief flooded through her as he moved aside.

'It's been a very hectic day at the end of a few dreadful weeks, and I guess you were the last straw. I saw the light on in here just when I thought I could at last escape. I'm sure those pot-plants will be put to very good use. It was very kind of you to bring them.' His tone was very gentle, as though she was after all only a very young girl in need of reassurance.

For some inexplicable reason she suddenly wanted to be that young girl who once would have gladly welcomed the comfort offered by this attractive man.

An old pain she thought had long disappeared for good clutched at her heart.

But attractive men couldn't be trusted. Hadn't she learnt that lesson well enough all those years ago?

And now there was no one of her own to turn to. Not even Gran. She was no longer available with her never-failing, patient, listening ear that had always heard more than the mere words. Ellena had always known as she had poured out her successes and failures that with Gran she would still be loved. . . accepted. . .never rejected. . .

She knew he had seen the tears that had trickled out on to her cheeks despite her best efforts at control, but felt too weary and full of pain to care that a perfect stranger was seeing her as she had not permitted anyone to see her for more years than she liked to think about. Even her grief these past weeks had been kept private.

'It's all right,' she murmured wearily. 'It's just that I've had a. . .a dreadful time too.'

Compassion filled the dark eyes, softening the strength of his angular face and jaw. He opened his mouth, but she knew she had to get out of there before she did dissolve into a storm of tears. She brushed past him, and strode hurriedly through the doorway and down the corridor, not stopping, even when he called after her.

She was thankful he didn't try to follow her as she brushed the falling tears impatiently away and hurried across the well lit car park. There had been too many tears shed these past weeks. It was more than time to

get heavily involved with her patients and staff again.
Through the years, hard work had always been a panacea for the disappointments and devastating heartaches
life had thrown her way. There had been so much hard
work that she had achieved her goal of becoming a
director of nursing much earlier than she had dared
hope. True, this was only a forty-bed unit so far. But
the builders had started on the next stage of the complex already, and who knew where it would end if Dr
Chris and Jean Hansen's dreams kept on eventuating?

At least Gran had been still there six months ago
to share the thrill of her being appointed to this brand-
new centre for rehabilitation care for elderly people,
to help them back to independence.

Her lips firmed as she drove away. And a success
she was determined to make of it too.

It was a very different woman who stood in front of
her mirror just over thirty-six hours later, making one
final assessment of her appearance, before leaving for
work. There were still dark shadows under the hazel
eyes, but the long, softly curling hair she so despised
was pinned neatly to the top of her head, adding at
least another five centimetres to her slender figure.
Comfortable shoes with a medium heel added further
to her height, and she knew with satisfaction she
looked every inch the director of nursing.

But a dragon lady? She scowled.

The unwelcome thought flashed into her mind that
she wished she had been at her best like this when she
had confronted that handsome man in her office!

Then she was annoyed with herself. That scene had
been replayed in her mind far too many times as it
was as she had cleaned out her flat, and unpacked!

Her carefully manicured fingers readjusted the collar of the crisp white blouse over the neckline of the well tailored navy blue jacket. She again blotted her carefully applied lipstick before glancing again at her watch.

It was only seven, but she had decided she needed to have plenty of time to look at the lists of patients and the staff roster before she went to the nurses' station for a verbal report. She dismissed with a frown the fleeting thought that her decision to start back on Sunday, a day early, was perhaps as much to make sure she was hopefully well established back in her position of authority before again encountering the stranger from two nights before.

It was a crisp spring morning, and the waters of Lake Macquarie were still and a deep blue as she climbed out of her car fifteen minutes later. Some keen sailors were already taking advantage of the glorious sunny morning after a cold winter, but the sails were limp, with barely a breeze to move them over the water.

She walked slowly towards the main entrance of Bensted House, taking note of the deserted construction site next to it. Chris had hoped the block of four one-bedroom residential units would be finished by now, but it was obvious there was still much to be done. Although it looked as though the windows and doors were in, so it must be completed to lock-up stage.

Six weeks ago there had been at least one of their elderly patients who would have benefited greatly by being able to try out how she could manage by herself in one of the units. Her overprotective family had needed to be convinced she could cope with living by herself again after her stroke.

She was still wondering what had happened to old Mrs Davis as she strode confidently in through the front door and along the corridor to her office. Her bunch of keys were in her hand ready to use, but the door was ajar. Surely that man had locked it for the weekend before he left the other night!

As she entered the room the first thing she saw was 'that man' standing at the window with his back to her.

'What are you doing in my office?' she asked sharply.

He visibly jumped and swung around. A large stream of water shot across the carpet from the watering can in his hand.

'I thought you might be back this morning,' he growled irritably. 'Now look what you've made me do!'

'I think you managed that very well all by yourself!' Ellena snapped.

She dropped her briefcase and handbag inside the door and hurried down the corridor a couple of rooms to the visitors' toilet. As she grabbed a handful of paper towelling, she realised she was trembling.

The last thing she had needed this morning, with six weeks to catch up on, was to again meet this. . .this disturbing man first thing. Who could he be? Surely not a visiting doctor! More likely a groundsman, by the watering can, the tight black jeans and the black T-shirt he was wearing this morning. But not too many gardeners and handymen wore well tailored suits on Friday evening at their place of work! Unless he had been visiting someone. A patient? Perhaps even a nurse?

For some reason that thought unexpectedly increased her anger.

He was lifting the cane wastepaper basket up as she

returned, and a trickle of water ran from it on to the carpet. She heard him mutter something indistinguishable, and as she rushed up and knelt down to mop up the water, he held the trickle over the top of the can he had placed on the floor.

'I'll mop that up,' he said curtly.

'You've already done enough damage,' Ellena snarled back very uncharacteristically. There was just something about this man that rattled her. 'And if you've been spraying my African violets from the top I'll kill you!'

He knelt down beside her and made a grab for the paper she was holding. She snatched it away. But before she could move, a strong brown hand had grabbed her wrist. His fingers were long and slender and a flash of electricity shot up her arm. She dropped the paper as through it was hot. He didn't seem to notice anything and just picked up the paper and continued to soak up the water that was rapidly spreading on the carpet.

'Of course I didn't spray the things. I took the spray off the spout. My mother did teach me that much about indoor plants.'

'I wish she'd also taught you to put water in the saucers of African violets. Just look what you've done!'

The anger in her voice made him look up and over to where she pointed to a stream of water running down the wall from the windowsill.

As she grabbed the watering can and rushed to empty the saucers, he muttered a word that made her wince as he stood up. Water dripped from the sodden paper in his hand.

'Oh, for goodness' sake! Why don't you run and get a couple of towels from the linen cupboard down the hallway? And drop that wretched paper! You're just ruining the carpet!' she roared.

'No way, madam! You can darned well get your own——'

A loud buzzing noise from the call system panel on the wall just outside the office cut across his furious words.

Someone was using the emergency code of three short bursts. Then the buzzer kept blaring as someone kept a finger on it.

CHAPTER TWO

ELLENA'S heart leaped as she automatically sprang forward. She nearly collided with the man as she flew through the doorway.

'Bathroom 1A!' he rapped out.

It barely registered with her that he knew the emergency code as together they rushed past the unoccupied large activity lounge room and down the corridor.

A tall woman in the blue registered nurse's uniform was coming rapidly from the other direction. Another stranger, thought Ellena a little grimly as they reached the bathroom entrance the same time. She noted a nurse in an enrolled nurse's uniform come racing out of a room at the far end of the corridor, pause as she saw them and then disappear again.

'Why, good morning, Ben,' the RN greeted him with a surprised look, and pushed past Ellena, barely glancing at her.

The loud buzzing of the alarm ceased and Ellena heard her exclaim with concern, 'Mrs Brown! Not again! Has she hurt herself, Ann?'

'I'm not sure, Sister,' a scared young voice said tearfully. 'She must have tried to stand up by herself when I raced off to get her sponge-bag.'

Ellena peered around the sister to see a large grey-haired lady sprawled on the floor of the doorway into the first cubicle, and a young enrolled nurse struggling to lift her into a sitting position.

'Don't move her, Nurse!' Ellena ordered sharply.

The RN swung around. 'Would you kindly stay out of this, please? We don't need the office staff to——'

'This is Miss Provis,' snapped Ben behind them as Ellena opened her mouth.

A startled expression crossed the woman's face, and dismay filled her eyes. 'I'm. . .I'm sorry. We. . .we weren't expecting you until tomorrow. I'm. . .I——'

Her voice stopped abruptly and some of the colour under her heavy make-up faded as Ellena looked steadily at her.

Warning bells went off inside Ellena's head. This woman was a little too dismayed that she had arrived unexpectedly. She tucked the thought away, and turned to the nurse still crouched beside the patient.

'Let's have a quick look and see if there's much damage before we try and move her, shall we, Nurse?' Ellena said firmly.

The RN moved aside, and Ellena waited while the nurse scrambled to her feet and out of the way.

'I. . .I overbalanced somehow, Nurse,' the large lady said a little breathlessly, 'but I don't think I've hurt meself.'

'Right hemi?' Ellena queried the RN softly as she tucked up her skirt a little and crouched down on the floor.

'That's right, love,' the patient answered her before the RN could speak. She pointed to the right arm she was half lying on that was still in its sling. 'Can't move the blasted thing much yet since the stroke, but me leg's not too bad.'

'Obviously not quite good enough yet to stand up from the toilet unassisted, Mrs Brown,' Ellena chided gently as she quickly examined her. Her fingers softly checked around a contusion on the patient's cheekbone from which a trickle of blood was seeping. 'You must have hit your face as you fell. Is it very sore?'

The patient winced 'I caught it a good wallop on the hand rail as I went down. But I was holding on to the other rail pretty tight with me good hand, and I didn't fall as heavy as I could have. Don't think there's much damage, love. If you could just heave me off this bad side. . .'

Ellena gently managed to place her hand behind the shoulder of the arm on the floor, and her other hand under the good arm.

'OK, you don't seem to have hurt your shoulder or arm. Tell me if there's any pain as I move you.'

Gently and slowly, with the assistance of Linda Terry, Ellena eased the heavy woman around until she could sit up and lean against the wall.

'Is your leg or hip painful anywhere?' Ellena asked as she continued her examination.

The woman was pale, but managed a slight smile at their anxious faces. 'Not really, Nurse. Probably get another woppin' bruise, I guess. Serve me right anyway for being such a silly old thing.'

Ellena noticed the RN glance anxiously at her watch, and wasn't at all surprised when she said in a rush, 'Do. . .do you think you could manage for a few minutes, Miss Provis? Breakfast will be here soon, and I. . .'

'And you have diabetics to attend to,' finished Ellena for her and smiled understandingly as she stood up. 'Perhaps the other RN on duty could help us and leave the nurses to finish getting the patients out of bed?'

There was a brief silence. The RN hesitated, but a deep voice said decisively, 'Sister Terry is the only RN on duty, I believe. I'll help you.'

Ellena scowled at him as he moved closer. Who on earth was this arrogant. . .? Then she realised what he had said.

'Only one RN on the morning shift? Someone off sick?'

Sister Terry suddenly looked at her defensively, and then shook her head. Ellena stared at her in amazement. Only one RN rostered!

'How many patients do you have in at the moment?'

'Thirty-six at present. We're expecting a couple of admissions tomorrow morning.' Ben's voice was crisp with authority.

Ellena glared at him in exasperation. 'You know a great deal about the place. Just who *are* you?'

'You haven't met Ben? Then you don't know——?'

'I'm quite capable of introducing myself.' His voice held the snap of authority. 'But not now, I think.'

Ellena followed his glance down to the patient on the floor. She had her eyes closed.

'How mobile is Mrs Brown, Sister?' Ellena queried abruptly.

There was another slight hesitation and then the sister said rapidly, 'She's been walking reasonably well with a pylon short distances for at least two weeks. Still lacks some co-ordination.'

There was something in the RN's voice that made Ellena look back at her quickly. The woman's pale blue eyes were now cold and resentful.

'Right. We'll manage. You'd better get on with your work. I'll catch up with what's happening later on,' Ellena ordered, aware that Mrs Brown had opened her eyes again and was now watching them all curiously.

The EN had already scurried away, and the sister merely nodded before dashing off.

'Now, Mrs Brown, I take it you came to the bath-room on that wheelchair?'

'Sure did. I told that young nurse I could use me pylon, but she just said, "Sister said". And that Sister's wrong anyway. Been using the pylon at home for weeks since me stroke. Only, I been having a few busters and Dr Hansen reckoned this place could help.' The patient sounded cross now.

Ellena's lips tightened, but all she said was, 'Well, I've been on leave, but I'm the director of nursing here, and if Dr Hansen thinks we'll be able to help you, I'm sure we will. Now,' she added briskly, 'have you ever been given any floor drill?' The woman looked blankly up at her, and she hastened to add, 'No matter, we'll do it now.'

'I know you're obviously very keen to get back into the swing of things, but I hardly think now is the time for doing what you call floor drill.' Ben's voice sounded angry. 'If you'd just move out of the way, I'll lift her up and——'

The furious glare Ellena turned on him made him stop abruptly. Thick black eyebrows shot up.

'If you also have something else to do, Mr. . . Mr. . . Ben, please feel free to do it! We can manage.' She forced herself to speak as calmly as she could for Mrs Brown's sake, but her flashing eyes left him in no doubt what she was thinking. 'Mrs Brown is going to have another lesson in independence.'

For a moment, those dark eyes flashed and his lips tightened, then suddenly he stilled.

'Uh-oh!'

The totally unexpected, murmured exclamation and the mischief that suddenly flashed into the dark eyes reminded her vividly of the night in the office.

Something responded again deep inside her as their eyes locked again. Then he seemed to check himself, and scowled.

Ellena forced her eyes away and pulled herself together with an effort. What on earth was it about this man?

'If you intend to help, would you please take off the foot supports on the wheelchair, and bring it nearer?'

She turned her back on him, and crouched down again. She was aware that he remained behind her as she briefly began to explain precisely what she wanted Mrs Brown to try and do, but a few moments later there was a faint clatter and then the chair was beside them. She ignored it and finished her instructions.

'So, do you think you can make an attempt at that? We'll go through this several other times in the next few days when you're not feeling as shaken.'

Ellena positioned the chair in front of Mrs Brown and locked on the wheel brakes carefully. At her instructions the patient managed to wriggle a little away from the wall so Ben could get on her left side.

'Now, this gentleman is *not* going to lift you. No matter how much he may want to. He is going to be only there in case you overbalance again.' She glared commandingly at him, and then glanced rapidly away as he unexpectedly glared back. 'OK, Mrs Brown, we'll support you if necessary, but I want you to do it by yourself if at all possible. Just take it slowly as I tell you exactly what to do.'

Step by step, Ellena gave clear instructions to get the woman on to her knees, her left hand on the chair to use as a support so that she could bring her strong knee up and position the foot correctly so she could start putting her weight on it. Ellena kept her own hand firmly on the woman's side to help balance her as she pushed herself up, also keeping a close eye on Ben's hand near the left shoulder. Fortunately the woman had enough control of her right leg to be able to position it properly with the minimum of assistance.

'Now, are you balanced on both feet? Good, then put your hand up on the arm of the chair, and do an ordinary chair transfer. Straighten up. Right knee locked? Then left foot around. Now right leg back. Keep the knee locked. Left again. Hand across to other side. Right leg. . .'

Ellena kept up the routine chant of instructions until the woman at last sat in the chair and beamed triumphantly up at them both.

'Well! I did that mostly meself! Me daughter'll never believe me!'

Ellena beamed back at her, but said as sternly as she could, 'You're far too heavy to expect your daughter to lift you. You did that so very well after the nasty fright you've had, and for the very first time too, that you can be assured you'll one day be able to do it all by yourself. As long as you haven't hurt yourself when you fell! But getting up will be one less thing for you to worry about.'

'I should think an even more important issue is to make sure you don't end up on the floor at all. Don't you think so, Mrs Brown?'

Ben had been busily replacing the feet supports, and as he glanced up at them there was disapproval in his voice and a frown on his face. The smile disappeared and the old faded eyes filled with worry. She opened her mouth, but Ellena stepped in quickly.

'I'm sure Dr Hansen is already looking into that. But now I think, if you've rested enough, you should finish at the hand-basin, we'll clean up that graze and go out to the dining-room.'

'Dining-room? Are we having breakfast there this morning?'

At the confusion in the old lady's voice, Ellena stared blankly at her and then looked at Ben enquiringly.

'I understand the patients have their breakfast in their rooms,' he said curtly, and then continued frowning as he studied her reaction.

She opened her mouth, changed her mind and said tightly as she started manoeuvring the wheelchair, 'Well, the bedroom it is. Which one are you in, Mrs Brown?'

'I'll see you in your office when you're ready, Miss Provis,' the deep baritone said commandingly as she moved past him.

Her back went rigid, but she bit her tongue. She very much needed to see *someone* to find out what had been happening here!

As she moved rapidly past several rooms, she noticed that only a couple of the occupants were out of bed, or even awake. Her anger gave way to concern. It was only about ten minutes before breakfast was scheduled to be served. Six weeks ago, the dining-room would already have been nearly full of all the patients except anyone who was not well enough.

After she had settled Mrs Brown in a chair beside her bed and returned the wheelchair, she hesitated, wondering if she should help the nurses or go straight back to the office. To her relief, a familiar tall nurse rushed out of a bedroom. She was frowning as she glanced at Ellena, and it was very gratifying to see her face light up.

'Miss Provis! Sister Terry said you were back!'

Such heartfelt relief was in her voice that Ellena's anxiety deepened. She had developed a good working relationship with as many of the staff as possible, but this particular enrolled nurse she'd had very little to do with.

'Why, thank you, Nurse Smythe,' she smiled at her faintly, 'and it's good to see a familiar face. I see you're very busy this morning.'

The frown returned to the pleasant face. 'We're frantically busy every morning now.'

'Maureen! Where the hell are you?' yelled an angry voice. A loud expletive followed. 'Sam's not up yet and the breakfast will be here any moment!'

The nurse must have seen the displeasure that sprang into Ellena's eyes. She shrugged and rolled her eyes, then murmured an apology and raced off.

There seemed little point in following her first instinct to reprimand the RN on the spot for speaking to staff like that. Offering assistance was also out when it was obvious the routine had been so changed that it would only add extra pressure on the staff's time to explain, so Ellena reluctantly started back to her office.

However, she yielded to temptation and made a detour through the empty dining-room to the kitchen. The atmosphere there too was tense, with the staff rushing frantically to finish serving up the food and placing trays on a large trolley.

The trolley was new. Ellena bit her lip as she saw it. There had only ever been need for a small trolley to take food to any patients too ill to get out of bed, which fortunately didn't happen very often, and no one with acute medical problems was admitted.

The kitchen staff were mainly weekend casuals, but

the cook in charge greeted her with such a similar look of relief to Maureen Smythe that after a brief greeting Ellena retreated again.

By the time she strode into her office, she was not only worried, but becoming angry. There had better be a good reason—a *very* good reason—why the carefully worked-out routine first put into operation when Macallister's had opened had been changed.

She had expected the man called Ben to be waiting in her office, but it was empty. The usual information on staff and patients had been left for the DON in their usual place on her desk, she was relieved to see. The red folder with the nursing staff roster was her first target.

She stared at the three names listed there for the morning shift with utter disbelief. If only one RN was on duty she had automatically expected at least one other nurse besides the two she'd seen! And only one nurse was scheduled to arrive at nine for the day shift. The evening shift that commenced at two-thirty was also understaffed. Thankfully the night staff roster had not been changed.

She sank on to her chair, and slowly opened the patients' folder. Some faint hope remained that perhaps the level of care of the majority of the patients was such that against all her experience three could be expected to cope.

A slight sound made her look up. Dark watchful eyes were studying her. She simply stared back at him, not realising that her dazed expression was responsible for the fact that his face darkened further as he moved forward.

'I've mopped up the water,' he said quietly.

'Th-thank you,' she stammered, realising with a little

shock that the events of the past three quarters of an
hour had driven all thought of that episode from her
mind. She took a deep breath and watched him warily
as he sank on to a chair beside the desk.

'Who are you? What's been happening here?' she
said sharply. 'This place is woefully understaffed this
morning! I rang up about four weeks ago to extend
my leave, and was assured everything was fine by the
administrator, Matthew Long. He said the acting
DON, Julie Newton, was coping very well.' She suddenly thought of something, and glanced down at the
sheets of paper in front of her. 'And why has Sister
Terry signed these reports? Where's Peggy?' she asked
with increasing alarm.

He looked at her accusingly. As she stared back at
him, the expression on his face changed, momentarily
showing a hint of uncertainty and a trace of bewilderment. Then his expression hardened again. At last he
sighed and ran a hand over the thick wavy hair.

'Peggy is Sister Howard, who was the acting deputy
director of nursing?'

She nodded briefly, 'She's the most senior sister on
the staff and agreed to act as deputy DON when Julie
had to become acting director when I. . .when I. . .'
She paused, and then asked anxiously '*Was* deputy,
did you say?'

Those black eyes searched her face again, and for
a moment she thought they seemed to pierce into her
carefully guarded heart. She felt the tension building
up in her by the moment. Her lips were dry and any
words she might have uttered dried up.

'But you knew she had left suddenly——'

'Left! Peggy Howard wouldn't leave!'

There was silence. A variety of expressions flicked

over his face as he stared at her. 'You don't know, do you?'

'Know? Know what?'

There was silence again as he studied her.

'Please. . .who are you?' Ellena whispered.

'I was given to understand that you had been told,' he muttered at last. 'I hardly know where to start.' He crossed one leg over the other and linked both hands around his knee. 'Yes, I'm afraid Sister Howard has left. The last I heard, she was specialling George Macallister in a private hospital.'

'Mr Macallister! Jean Hansen's father!'

At her exclamation, he added quickly, 'He had another stroke just over three weeks ago, and is still in hospital. The latest word is that he's recovering reasonably well.'

'Oh, the poor dear! And poor Jean, too,' Ellena said in a choked voice.

He was watching her intently as he said slowly, 'And poor Chris. He's very close to his father-in-law.'

Their gazes locked, each recognising the other's compassion and pain for good people. Then he frowned again, as though something perplexed him.

'You. . .you know Dr Hansen?' asked Ellena hesitantly.

'I was best man at their wedding. I've known Chris since we were kids.'

He uncrossed his legs and straightened. His expression changed again. That finger and thumb caressed the moustache.

Caressed?

Ellena shivered.

Suddenly the gesture seemed very familiar. As though she had known him a lot longer than a couple of brief encounters. Her first reaction was that she wished he'd stop doing that! It stirred that innermost part of her that had recognised before how attractive he was.

Then, unexpectedly, she somehow was sure that he smoothed that moustache unconsciously while choosing his words. Her hands clenched, and she braced herself as he started to speak again in a brisk voice.

'I'm Ben Nicoletti. Chris rang me when everything seemed to happen to them at once. Within forty-eight hours, his father-in-law was in hospital, he'd lost the acting deputy DON because they needed her to special Mr Macallister, the acting DON collapsed at work from not giving in to an attack of influenza soon enough before it developed into pneumonia, and then Matthew had a heart attack!'

Ellena was looking at him with absolute horror. Then she caught her breath as contempt filled the eyes that stared back at her.

'And his director of nursing had just extended her holidays! *And* refused to come back to help out!'

Ellena jumped to her feet. She put both hands on the desk to steady her trembling body as her brain reeled. 'What. . .what did you say? Refused? How could I. . .? I didn't know. . .'

Suddenly he cut across her confusion as he stood up also. He seemed to tower over her.

I was right, she thought numbly, he can be intimidating.

Then years of training came to her aid. She straightened. Her chin went up. 'Are you accusing me of. . .of. . .?'

Words failed her. Just what was he accusing her of? Of being unprofessional? Of turning her back on an emergency she had known nothing about? Of being self-indulgent? Heartless?

'I just find it incredible that you refused to put off your holiday and return to help out.' His eyes were black pits of smouldering anger and condemnation, and then he looked down at the folders on the desk. 'We were thankful that Julie Newton had managed only the week before to employ someone who was willing and capable of taking over at such short notice as acting DON. And she's been managing without a deputy, too. I hope you take that into consideration if you find she hasn't been able to achieve your standards.'

He moved towards the door.

'Wait!' Ellena's voice sounded strangled. 'Where are you going? Is Matthew all right? Where's Julie now? And you. . .you still haven't told me what you do here!'

She knew what he was going to say, even as he looked scornfully at her.

'I'm the new administrator, and filling in wherever I can for Chris until he gets back. Matthew's OK now, but he won't be back for a long time, if ever. He's waiting for a coronary artery by-pass operation. And where am I going? It's Sunday. I'm off home to get ready for church.' His voice was cold and curt. 'I only decided to come in after I had made enquiries and had confirmed my suspicion that the intruder I disturbed in this office was the missing DON come sneaking back. I came in because, from what I've been warned about the dragon lady, I suspected you might want to surprise the staff a day early. And don't you dare give those poor kids a rough time or. . .or. . .you'll have me to reckon with!' He swallowed convulsively, visibly controlling the rising fury she heard in his voice. 'Even if it's only to be expected of a dragon lady! I'll be back at work tomorrow.'

'But. . .but you can't just throw all. . .all these accusations at me and. . .and walk off!'

'I can't?'

The sarcastic smile that twitched his lips was so different from the genuine one at their first meeting, and those molten black eyes filled with so much fury and scorching disdain that Ellena could only watch helplessly as he turned his back and marched out of the office.

CHAPTER THREE

ELLENA slumped back on to her chair, pressing both hands unbelievingly to her mouth.

Perhaps I should have somehow made the time to rest more on my 'holiday', she thought bitterly, as the familiar throb commenced of one of her all too frequent headaches.

Yesterday she had kept herself very busy, trying to keep at bay the memories she was finding so hard to cope with. Now what she had gone through during the last few weeks began to swamp her. She shuddered and closed her eyes tightly against the burning behind them.

Her grandmother had been found early in the morning by a neighbour and raced to hospital. She had been barely conscious in Coronary Care when Ellena had at last arrived, but had managed to smile as Ellena kissed her and then frowned at the tears that had trickled down her white cheeks at the change in the lined, beloved face. Their hands had clung, and then the old lady had given a sigh and relaxed, going to sleep peacefully.

That first week she had hardly left her grandmother's side. The old lady had been reasonably bright and very happy to have Ellena's constant company as she had very slowly recovered. But during the second week she had insisted Ellena go and help the neighbours who were milking the cows for them on the farm that had been owned by the family for generations.

She had been doing so well that Ellena had agreed, and had even rung Macallister's to let them know she would be back the next week. But then had come that nightmarish evening, when there had been that last dreadful seizure. Ellena had watched helplessly as the cardiac arrest team had swung into action. All the times she had been part of such a team in the past had still not prepared her for the horror of at last realising everything humanly possible had been done to no avail. She'd walked in a haze of anguish away from the hospital for the last time.

That numbness had still been with her when she had rung Macallister's. Matthew must not have written down the first two weeks as compassionate leave, or told anyone that she had rushed to offer to take her four weeks' annual leave instead of more compassionate leave when he had at first hesitated. She had known that with the Hansens away also it would be difficult, but had known she needed the time away desperately.

Suddenly she wished she had told him about her grandmother's death instead of mumbling something about still being needed, but somehow she had been still too shocked herself to make it any more real by putting it into words.

I wonder what kind of a holiday they think I've had, she thought. Swanning off to the Gold Coast? Perhaps some romantic tropical isle on the Great Barrier Reef? The hours spent outdoors on the farm had certainly tanned her skin to a golden brown, but that was the result of sheer hard work.

The shrill summons of the telephone brought her back to the present. Tears were trickling down her face. She impatiently brushed them aside and reached automatically to pick up the phone, but the ringing stopped and the red light flashed as someone else answered it on another line.

She frowned. Someone must have been right next to it at the nurses' station. Instead of supervising breakfast, she thought grimly.

The phone rang again. Ellena waited a moment and then snatched the receiver.

'Miss Provis speaking.'

There was a pause, and then a voice said coldly, 'So you are back!'

'Julie, is that you? I just heard you've been sick. Are you OK?'

There was another pause, and then she heard Julie ask slowly, 'What do you mean, you've *just* heard?'

Ellena groaned. 'Oh, no! Not you too! Someone called Ben Nicoletti has just accused me of all kinds of dreadful things. Why didn't anyone ring and tell me? For heaven's sake, I was only two hours' drive away!'

'But. . .but I was told you'd been contacted, but that you refused point-blank to cut your holiday short!' Julie's voice was warmer, but sounded bewildered.

'Who told you that?'

'Why, Linda Terry, when she came to see me in hospital.'

Ellena's hand clenched on the phone. 'Then Linda Terry was mistaken,' she said grimly. 'I'm still not sure I know what's been happening. Disaster on disaster from what that. . .that man told me. Are you still too sick for me to call in later today and catch up?'

'That would be rather difficult I think,' Julie said dryly, 'even for you. I'm over two hours away at my parents' home in Sydney.'

'Sydney! Whatever happened, Julie? That. . .that man just said you'd collapsed with pneumonia because you wouldn't stop working while you had the flu. Surely you. . .you. . .'

'I'd have more sense?' Julie acknowledged. 'Yes, well, it wasn't quite like that. When I woke up I thought it was only a nasty cold, and as Matthew hadn't been very well either I went in. But by lunchtime I was feeling so groggy I knew I should go home to bed. But because Peggy had gone, things were behind. You. . .you heard about George Macallister?'

'Ben Nicoletti just told me.'

'I still can't understand. . .' Julie's voice hesitated for a moment, and then continued firmly before Ellena could speak, 'Anyway, I finished a couple of important reports, and I'd just told poor old Matthew I was off home when I fainted. And besides,' she continued indignantly, 'the bronchial asthma that developed that night only turned to pneumonia later.'

'Julie!' Ellena said in horror.

'Well, I'm getting on fine now. Just a bit shaky in the legs since I left hospital a few days ago, and——'

'Hospital! A few days ago? But that means you must have been there for over three weeks! Julie, what on earth. . .?'

There was silence for a moment, and then Julie's voice said softly, 'My phone was out of order, and I was too sick to get over to the neighbours. They. . . they found me unconscious the next day.'

Ellena was aware of the too ready tears again filling her eyes. A sudden spasm of fear gripped her. She too lived alone. In a solitary flat. With no one except neighbours to. . .

'Oh, Julie, I'm so sorry,' she managed to say huskily through the dread that gripped her.

'Well, it was fortunate that Linda Terry was only

too happy to take over. Apparently the other RNs were very reluctant to give acting DON a go.' She paused, and her voice changed. 'Ellena, there's something I must tell you straight away. My. . .my parents want me to get another job closer to home. And. . . and there's someone special down here I've just met. . .'

Ellena closed her eyes, dismay filling her to an even deeper degree as she knew what the faltering voice was trying to tell her.

'And so you won't be back,' she said sadly.

'I'm. . .I'm sorry, Ellena. The doctor insists I need at least another couple of weeks to rest, and I thought you should know so you can replace me as soon as possible,' Julie finished with a rush. 'I'm sending off my written resignation today.'

Ellena tried to say all the right things, and must have succeeded, as Julie sounded much happier and relieved by the time she rang off.

She stared grimly at the phone. Julie had been an excellent deputy. Her attitude to the work had matched her own so closely, and they had worked so well together that she knew it would be very difficult to replace her. And now she didn't even have her to talk to about the past few weeks! And then she wished she had at least asked her what she knew of Matthew and George.

Deep down, she knew she had also been dying to pour out a host of questions about Mr Ben Nicoletti. But as far as she knew, Julie might not even have met the new administrator, and she had still felt too raw from his attack to mention him again.

She thought for a few moments and then picked up the phone, only to replace it with disappointment when no one answered at the Hansens' residence next door. She didn't even know which hospitals George and Matthew were in. Unless they'd already been discharged, like Julie! She tried Matthew's home number, but drew a blank there.

With a sigh, she went over to the filing cabinet. At least she could find out something about what had happened to the patients while she was away.

She opened the discharge book first. It had been meticulously kept by Julie's neat hand. In one sense the records duplicated the official computer record kept by the office staff, but Julie had wholeheartedly agreed that they needed to add their own comments.

There were not many surprises the first couple of weeks. She had expected the double amputee, old Bob Thompson, would be ready for home, and noted that Julie had written, 'Still some doubt about carers' ability to cope. Needs follow-up in a couple of weeks,' and wondered briefly what had happened with his timid daughter and her domineering husband.

She turned the page and found that after a couple of entries in an almost indecipherable hand, the rest of the pages were blank. She flipped open the follow-up folder but nothing at all had been written in there except the comment by Julie that Bob Thompson was managing very well at home by himself. Surely there had been more discharges and follow up during the previous four weeks!

She checked back to see if Mrs Davis had been discharged. When she drew a blank, she frowningly reached for the pile of daily reports. There had been several discharges, but not one had been written up in the discharge book.

One of the prices of no deputy, she thought grimly.

And knew she wasn't at all convinced someone could not have been at least temporarily employed before this to fill the gap.

To her intense disappointment Mrs Davis was down as awaiting nursing home placement. They had tried so hard with her, and Dr Hansen had agreed when she had told him she believed the indomitable old lady needed another few weeks of consistent training and she would at least qualify for hostel accommodation if they had to agree with the family that she could not cope at home. At the hostel she would have been able to have her own room and quite a few of her personal belongings as well as maintaining much more independence than was possible at most nursing homes.

She checked the admissions diary to see who was expected the next morning. Again, nothing. That was too much! She hoped there was at least some information at the nurses' station! Even more disturbing was the fact that there appeared to be no waiting list for admissions, and there were spare beds.

After making several notes from the current patients' brief records of things she wanted to check for herself from their charts, she then returned the folders to the filing cabinet and rather reluctantly opened the staff drawer.

She looked at the folder marked 'Linda Terry, RN', and then slowly pulled it out and took it to the desk. Her letter of application was dated a few days before Ellena had left, so might have arrived in the mail that very day. They had needed at least one more RN, and no doubt Julie had breathed a sigh of relief.

Ellena studied the folder's contents carefully, and then frowned as she tapped her Biro thoughtfully on the desk. She glanced at her watch. It was still too early to do her usual round of the patients. However. . .

She set her lips firmly, decisively put away the folder, picked up her notes and made her way briskly to the wards.

The domestic staff were busily stacking trays back on the trolley, and glanced up at her as she reached them. She smiled pleasantly as she paused, even as her eyes passed over the trays. Quite a bit of food seemed to be left on them. She noticed one cup of tea looked as though it had not even been touched, and several small packets of processed bran had not been opened—a very important part of the diet of many elderly people! A boiled egg also sat untouched on another tray.

Maureen Smythe raced out of a room carrying a tray. 'Sorry! Mrs Davis took longer to feed than——' She saw Ellena watching her and stopped abruptly. Then she clattered the tray on to a rack and said hurriedly, 'Did you want Sister Terry for a round, Miss Provis? She's still giving out the medications.'

And that was another thing, thought Ellena angrily. It was so much faster giving out medications when the patients were together in the dining-room! As well as again seeming more like home than a hospital ward.

'No, no, not just yet,' she managed to say calmly. 'I realise it's a bad time. I'll just check out the paper-work first.' She gestured with her hand and added, 'Is that Mrs Davis's room now?'

'Yes, she's sharing with Mrs Brown.'

'And she can't feed herself any more?'

Ellena knew how much that loss of independence would have upset the indomitable old lady.

'Er. . .that's right. . .' Maureen paused, and then added hurriedly, 'At least when she's still in bed. She can't manage without making a mess, and takes forever.'

She avoided looking at Ellena, and after a moment Ellena murmured, 'Then perhaps you should make sure she isn't in bed in the future, Nurse.'

Before her anger was taken out on the unfortunate girl who must after all only be following orders, Ellena swung away and continued on to the nurses' station.

Of course the handicapped old lady could not manage propped up in bed! she thought furiously. This having breakfast in bed was hopeless, especially for patients with poor muscle co-ordination skills and those with the use of only one hand. And who were supposed to be learning independence at meal time as part of their rehabilitation.

She passed a corridor and noticed the medication trolley halfway along. A harsh voice echoed down to her, and she frowned. Another thing high on her list of priorities was the need to check the ex-acting DON's way of speaking to patients as well as staff!

When she picked up the first patient's chart, she found another change. The observation and medication sheets were no longer on it. Her mouth tightened as she checked a few more. Put back on the end of the beds again! Once again taking away the homely atmosphere they had tried so hard to create in the rooms. Something else to be corrected. Besides, the patients were hardly ever in their rooms during the day, and it had proven much easier to keep all charts together in the trolley, and the medication sheets in a separate folder.

Ellena had finished studying the charts of patients admitted while she had been away, and was looking thoughtfully at Mrs Davis's history notes when Linda

Terry arrived. She looked taken aback to see the DON sitting at the desk.

'Don't worry about me yet, Sister,' Ellena said politely. 'I'll do a quick round when you're ready. There are still a couple of things I can check here, and we can wait until the day-shift nurse arrives.'

'Oh, I can do a round now. The girls can continue with the showers. The sooner you have a grasp of what's been happening, the better.'

Linda Terry had made a quick recovery, but her smile didn't quite reach her eyes, although her voice oozed with friendliness.

It would be difficult to hand back the place she had been in charge of for so many weeks, Ellena thought charitably, determined to give her the benefit of the doubts that had crept into her mind as she read the résumé included in her position-application information.

'Great,' she said cheerfully. 'I'll put these charts back in the trolley, and we'll start.'

Several of the long-term patients greeted Ellena enthusiastically. But as she chatted briefly to them she noticed that they treated Linda with reserve, and a couple never even acknowledged she was there.

Patients did become fond of certain nurses, Ellena knew. She herself had always had the knack of establishing good relationships with most of her patients over the years, and even though administration now took up so much of her time, she had made a determined effort to know personally each patient.

But she gradually became more and more perturbed by the attitude of most of the patients towards Linda herself, and even more upset by the abrupt way several of the more recent patients expressed that they were unhappy with their treatment.

'Doc said you'd have me walking on a pylon within a few days when he admitted me here,' one distinguished-looking man complained, 'and that was nearly two weeks ago.' He glared accusingly at them from his bed. 'And I'm not even out of bed this morning yet! At least at the public hospital the staff would have showered me by now.'

Sr Terry looked up from studying his chart, and said placatingly, 'Now, now, you know you are still having sessions on the circo-electric bed, Mr. . .er. . .' she looked at the name tag above the bed '. . .Mr Harrington. And the physiotherapist hasn't started you on a tripod yet.'

Ellena bit her tongue. Why hadn't the nursing staff started him themselves, if Chris had said he was ready? There had never been enough time for the physiotherapist to do all that was needed.

'Haven't even seen any blessed physio,' the man said angrily. 'And I hate that stupid tilt-table thing. And you left me on it for well over half an hour yesterday!'

Ellena glanced sharply at Linda. The woman's hands were resting on the end of the bed, but suddenly she moved jerkily, and Ellena frowned as she noticed the distinct tremor in her hand as she reached for the charts at the end of the bed.

A slight trace of pink stained Sister Terry's cheeks and she avoided looking at Ellena as she said with a false laugh, 'Now, Mr Harrington, you know that's not quite so. It probably only seemed like that, and. . . and. . .'

'And we'll sort it all out as soon as possible, sir,' Ellena said briskly as Linda stumbled to a stop, and she saw Mr Harrington ready to fling more words at them.

But it was perhaps the look of defeat on Mrs Davis's face that upset Ellena the most.

'They say it's useless to keep trying, Ellena,' she said sadly in her slurred voice. 'Might as well go to a nursing home and be done with it.'

'Oh, Pat, I'm so sorry, love. But you've certainly given it your best shot.'

'Have I?'

The old lady's head drooped, and when she looked up, it was Sister Terry's face she peered at. Tears welled up in the faded eyes, and then they turned to Ellena with an expression in them that she could not quite understand.

Ellena hesitated and glanced at the RN as she moved impatiently. There was a set expression on her face. No, not a set look, Ellena suddenly realised. It was hard, unsympathetic.

'Look, I'll come back later, and you can tell me all about it,' she said hurriedly as she handed Mrs Davis a tissue, and patted her on the hand before moving out of the room.

'I can't understand the change in her,' Ellena said thoughtfully. 'There's no suggestion in her notes that she could have had an extension of her CVA.'

'Oh, I think she just couldn't be bothered any longer. Besides, her family don't want her to go home. Insist she couldn't manage by herself,' Linda dismissed the old lady abruptly as she walked into the next room.

Ellena tensed, and then bit her lip before following her, reminding herself that after all this. . .this woman must have helped out considerably the past few weeks in admin. She decided there and then to find out a bit more where Sister Terry was coming from before she said what she would very much like to!

There were only a couple more patients and she spoke briefly to them before pushing the trolley of charts back to the desk.

Linda had been very co-operative, very friendly. But it had become more and more obvious to Ellena that she did not know a great deal about most of the patients, although she was trying her utmost to ingratiate herself with the DON.

'Right, Sister Terry. I've held you up long enough. I'll go and get Mrs Davis up and supervise her shower and dressing,' Ellena said briskly.

'Oh, my goodness, you don't have to do that!' Sister Terry sounded scandalised.

'It will give us an opportunity to have the talk I promised her,' Ellena said firmly, and moved quickly away.

She didn't think it necessary to add she also wanted to assess for herself one of her favourite patients.

When she had made sure a bathroom was free she marched back to Mrs Davis. 'Right, Pat! Let's get you up.'

The old lady was startled and then pathetically delighted as Ellena found her slippers and dressing-gown. But then she sat there after Ellena had placed them on the bed, obviously waiting for Ellena to put them on her.

'Getting lazy in your old age, are you?' teased Ellena with a grin. 'You put them on while I get your clothes out.'

There was no answering smile, and Ellena watched from the corner of her eye with dismay as the gnarled old fingers of one hand fumbled pathetically. In the end, without a word, Ellena went through the drill again that had been taught to Mrs Davis at least three months before. Gently she showed her the technique of first easing the useless, paralysed arm through the left sleeve with her good hand, then pushing the good arm through before gathering up the gown and pushing and pulling it over the head.

Ellena looked around the room for the old wooden quad stick the old lady had used with its distinctive padded handle.

'If you're looking for my pylon, its probably still out in the lounge room. They take me to my room on the wheelchair now,' Mrs Davis said softly.

Ellena looked at her sharply, but there was so much misery in the old eyes that without a word she raced off to get a wheelchair. When she returned she was thankful that at least the old lady could still manage to hook her good leg under her weak one and manage to swing them over the side of the bed and scramble up herself. The bed-to-chair transfer went very well also, as did the transfer to the shower chair once they reached the bathroom.

'Now off with your dressing-gown and nightie while I regulate the water temperature.'

That was managed reasonably well, but during the rest of the time it became more and more obvious that the old lady was now used to having nearly everything done for her.

Ellena chatted away, slipping in constant instructions, but on the whole Mrs Davis remained unusually quiet for the once talkative old lady. There were a few references to her protective family, but 'Sister Terry said. . .' featured in far too many of her responses for Ellena's peace of mind.

Even worse for her peace of mind was the occasional

references to 'that wonderful young man, Ben' who apparently had spent quite a bit of time with the old lady. In fact, it was only when speaking about him that Mrs Davis became even the slightest bit animated.

'Such a handsome young man,' she said with the first real smile Ellena had seen. 'And so successful, too. I've known him since he was only a small lad, you know. His dad would be real proud of him, the way he kept the business going after his death. Built up the family's electronics business when it nearly went under in these difficult times. It was very fortunate for us that his younger brother had just taken over before Matthew. . .' The smile disappeared abruptly, and she added softly, 'Poor Matthew. . .and poor George Macallister. So sad. All that hard work to get back on his feet after his first stroke, and now. . .'

'I'm sure George is doing reasonably well again,' Ellena said swiftly, hoping desperately she was right. 'And he would be the first to say all that effort to be able to go home was more than worthwhile. Now, what about putting on your own shoes and stockings!'

A dark shadow had chased away the brief spurt of animation on the old wrinkled face. With a sinking heart, Ellena realised how very depressed she had become as she watched her battle to put on stockings and give up far too quickly. She looked up at Ellena, and a large tear rolled down her pale cheek.

'If only I had more sleep at night! But those sisters just won't give me more sleeping tablets,' Mrs Davis complained querulously.

'But you know that Dr Hansen doesn't like you to have any tablets at night unless you absolutely have to,' Ellena said gently. 'Don't you remember? You're more likely to be too shaky when you have to use the

commode during the night and risk a fall. That is, if
you are able to wake up in time to avoid an accident!
And you were doing very well before, love.'

'But Sister Terry said I wasn't getting enough sleep
with only five or six hours, and so I've had to have a
nap after lunch each day.'

There it was again, 'Sister Terry said. . .' thought
Ellena with disgust.

By the time Mrs Davis was ready to leave the bathroom, Ellena was very upset. She knew the once
indomitable old lady had simply given up.

With apparently considerable assistance by a certain
incompetent sister, Ellena thought with increasing
anger and frustration.

CHAPTER FOUR

WHEN Ellena at last returned to her office it was well past her own lunch break. With great self-control she carefully closed the door behind her instead of slamming it as she would dearly have loved to do to relieve her feelings!

Her head was really throbbing now. She fumbled in her bag for some paracetamol, and when she had swallowed them stood for a moment with her hands clenched and her eyes closed. Then she grabbed her cut lunch, and headed for the door.

The phone rang.

There was only a slight pause in her stride. Then she continued even faster out of the room, out the front door and towards her favourite spot, hidden by a bank of gloriously blooming azaleas from the wards and looking out over the lake.

She felt completely drained from the restraint she had exercised since starting the round with Linda Terry, and badly needed to breathe the tangy salt air wafting off the gently rippling water. Taking a deep breath, she let the tranquil beauty of blue water and blue sky begin to relax her.

Being pleasant to Linda Terry had ended up taxing every ounce of patience she'd had! No matter how experienced the woman was in other specialised areas of nursing, it was obvious she knew little about the principles behind a geriatric rehabilitation programme such as operated at Macallister's. That had happened with another RN here also, but that woman had at least recognised the fact and not been too arrogant to learn! And, even worse, it was very obvious that Linda Terry had never even been in charge of a ward before, so why on earth had she offered to be acting DON?

Even as she silently congratulated herself on her restraint, Ellena's lips twitched grimly as she realised how close she had come to losing her self-control a few moments ago when she had said firmly, 'Sister Terry, I'm going to lunch now. When you have handed over to the afternoon staff, I'd like to see you in my office, please.'

And that. . .that woman had dared to simper and say, 'Oh, I'm sure you don't need me to help you settle in any more. I wanted to get away early today as I'm on days off, so I'm afraid it won't be convenient to——'

'Be in my office by three o'clock, Sister Terry, or you may not have a job to come back to after your days off!' Ellena had heard herself snap through gritted teeth before turning abruptly away from the look of shock that had chased the smirk off the woman's face.

Ellena would never have believed that a place could change as much as this one had in such a handful of weeks! But something had to be done about it. And done very fast!

After finally settling Mrs Davis in a chair where she could watch television, Ellena had helped the EN, Ann White, to make several beds, much to the young girl's obvious astonishment. She had been nervous, but seemed capable enough, and Ellena liked her kind, understanding approach to the patients, who obviously thought the world of her.

Linda had really looked down her nose at the sight

of the DON making beds! Ellena had noted grimly that she had not seen the RN make one bed, just race patients far too quickly in and out of the bathrooms for any training in showering and dressing skills.

Ellena had with difficulty maintained a friendly façade during the rest of her time on the ward, not feeling at all guilty as she had egged Linda on to show her true feelings towards several of the patients, including Mrs Davis, and had not failed to see the self-satisfied smile that had twisted Sister Terry's lips several times.

As the morning had worn on, it had become more and more obvious how badly the place was under-staffed for adequate rehabilitation techniques to be implemented. It might have just been adequate for a nursing home, but even the most dedicated nurses would have found it impossible to spend anywhere near enough time teaching rehab techniques. Besides, the patients needed a lot of time to be as independent as possible with all the activities of daily living, or ADL as they called it in their paperwork.

When asked about the staff levels, Linda had said, 'My goodness, I caught so many nurses, and even RNs, just standing watching patients do things for themselves that I very quickly realised that we were grossly over-staffed.'

Before Ellena had been able to say a word, she had added very proudly, 'When I told Ben, he ordered me to make whatever changes were necessary. He was very pleased with the savings to his budget.'

As she remembered how flabbergasted she had felt at such a blatant display of ignorance of the difference between a nursing home and this complex, Ellena groaned, thinking of all the things she could have said.

That woman had been so sure she had been doing the place a favour that Ellena had found herself momentarily speechless.

And the administrator had 'ordered' the acting DON?

Ellena had ended up saying rather feebly something about how hard it must have been getting staff to take holidays or cuts in hours, and had even attempted to commiserate with her about the difficulties she must have experienced doing the rosters.

But she had only been met with a rather blank, uncomprehending look.

'Oh, no, once I had the *correct* number of staff worked out that I needed for the level of care required, it was a breeze,' Linda had said confidently, and then her face had lit up as she added, 'Ben and I became very close while we were working it all out together. He's an excellent administrator!'

When she had helped the staff move the patients into the dining-room for lunch, it had quickly become very obvious to Ellena that Linda herself really knew very little about rehabilitation techniques, especially simple chair transfers, and the drill of walking patients with frames, as well as other aids like the four-legged wooden pylons favoured by Dr Hansen. She also noticed that, more often than not, Linda used wheel-chairs instead of walking mobile patients, which had always been frowned on severely.

Ellena sat down on a park bench at the edge of the grass close to the sand and forced herself to swallow a few mouthfuls of lunch. Her appetite had deserted her the past few weeks, but she knew there would be much work to do before her next break.

Then she reluctantly took her notebook out of the

pocket of her jacket and checked scribbled notes she
had been taking all morning. Some time later, still
deep in thought, she at last went for a short walk along
the water's edge.

As she looked across at the Hansens' house, she
realised the large old brick place appeared to be
deserted. There was an air of neglect about the yard.
The blinds were drawn, and she realised that they must
have been away for some time. It was obvious the dear
old man, Mr Macallister, who lived with his daughter
and son-in-law, must have been hospitalised somewhere away from the area.

Oh, why hadn't that Ben Nicoletti stayed long
enough to tell her what was happening?

She'd noticed on the patients' charts that Chris's
registrar at the John Hunter Hospital in nearby
Newcastle, young Dr James Gill, had been looking
after the patients the last few weeks, which in itself
was extremely unusual for the dedicated geriatrician.
She had learnt very early after she had started working
for them that he had always given top priority to his
wife, but had still very rarely missed his regular rounds
at Macallister's. And he had often popped in to see
new patients even more than that.

She thought about the young couple, remembering how she had suffered several pangs when she had
first realised the depth of the loving relationship
between them.

If only Howard had loved her like that! But the
man she had once loved, and whom she had thought
returned her love enough to marry her, had proved to
be nothing more than a con man, a scoundrel.

Unexpectedly, Ben's face filled her mind. As it had
been when he had been upset because he thought he

had made her cry. It had been a long time since a
man had seen past her cool, professional façade. Deep
down, she knew that no man had ever had quite the
same effect on her as Ben Nicoletti had. Certainly
Howard never had!

Abruptly, she tried to cut off her thoughts and
turned back to Macallister's. After all, that dreadful
business with Howard had all happened so long ago.
Nearly ten years. And that in itself made a spasm of
pain shoot through her. She had only been twenty
then. Almost finished her nurse's training. And next
birthday she would be thirty. Thirty!

That she had never married again had always
grieved Gran.

Gran.

Determinedly Ellena pushed her own problems from
her mind as she entered through a side entrance and
went to the staff-room. After she had freshened up, she
made a cup of coffee which she took back to her office.

Ben Nicoletti was waiting for her.

And he was sitting in her chair. At her desk!

And he was reading her folders obviously taken from
the open filing cabinet drawer!

Those dark, unforgettable eyes, framed by eyelashes
which were far too long and thick for a man, watched
her pause momentarily in the doorway. They gleamed
appreciatively as she steadily advanced to his side of
the desk, not taking her eyes from his.

Ellena was proud of her steady hand as she managed
not to allow her instant inner trembling to be revealed
as she placed the cup on the desk without spilling
a drop.

'Good afternoon, Mr Nicoletti.'

'Good afternoon, Matron Provis.'

She continued to hold his mocking gaze steadily for a moment, despite the anger stirring within her.

Then she said smoothly, 'I'm afraid you are very out of touch, Mr Nicoletti. We no longer use "matron". Miss Provis is quite sufficient, thank you. And now, if I may sit down at *my* desk, please?'

He held her gaze without moving for several moments, as though he sensed the turmoil of conflicting emotions that she was battling to suppress. At last he moved abruptly, closing the folder. As he stood up, he picked it up with another one on the desk and strolled casually over to the filing cabinet.

She sat down and clenched her hands tightly together in her lap to try and stop their trembling. Her own name had been on the front of the folder. She had not been able to see the name on the other, but he replaced them both in the staff drawer before closing it slowly.

'I thought a new administrator would already be familiar with the details of his DON's résumé and appointment particulars.' She was proud of her steady, even voice.

'There were a couple of things I needed to double-check,' he said abruptly.

Without asking permission, he picked up a chair against the far wall and sat beside the desk. He then leaned back, linked both hands behind his head and stared thoughtfully at her.

She refused to look away, although she felt the warm colour flooding her cheeks at his frank appraisal. He was once again wearing his dark suit without a tie, and now the coat had fallen open as he leaned back on the chair. His fitted shirt was made of fine white cotton and muscles rippled across his chest as he moved.

'Certain things I know about you don't add up with

the glowing references in that folder,' he said at last. Then he frowned suddenly and dropped his hands. One went to his moustache before he added, 'Especially the one from a Reverend Mr Telford.'

Ellena took a deep breath. Her anger increased. Mr Telford had been the chaplain of the church-owned nursing home in Sydney. She had been the deputy director of nursing there for two years before she had applied for this position.

Suddenly she found she could not hold his assessing gaze, and reached to pick up her cup of coffee. She look a sip, holding it in both hands, wishing the warmth of the cup could take away the coldness that was settling on her heart.

'Did you make it in time to church?' she asked after it became obvious that he was not going to clarify what he meant.

Sheer pride refused to let her ask what he thought he knew about her!

His eyes narrowed, but he answered politely, 'Yes, thank you. We enjoyed the service very much.'

We?

For some stupid reason she had not thought of him with a wife. Perhaps he even had a small boy with those same dark eyes.

A shiver passed through her. She carefully placed the cup back on the table, and after a moment she looked up at him steadily.

'What a shame the sermon wasn't from the Gospel of Saint Matthew, chapter seven, verse one.'

A startled expression crossed his face as he stared at her. Then unexpectedly an appreciative grin brought out the far too attractive dimple.

'Now, if my memory serves me right, that sermon

would be all about judging others, right?'

She just looked at him silently, hoping her surprise at his knowledge did not show in her face, and a little ashamed at having yielded to the unworthy urge of letting him know she was not a stranger to church life herself.

The amusement in his eyes slowly faded.

'What did you come back today for?' she asked abruptly.

'Why do you think?'

'To continue insulting me?'

'I'm sorry.' He looked rueful as he saw her surprise. 'I can only assure you that I don't normally behave as I did this morning.'

He ran a hand through his thick wavy hair. The feeling that was becoming all too familiar when she was in this man's striking presence stirred deep within her.

'You were right,' he said abruptly. 'It wasn't fair of me to throw all those things at you and then leave. I shouldn't have stormed out of here like that.'

She remained silent from sheer astonishment. In her experience, strong, masculine men like Ben rarely, if ever, apologised so spontaneously.

'I don't know what on earth got into me!' He paused. A puzzled look crossed his face. 'I realised as soon as I reached the car that I had let you get to me,' he added with a touch of irritation.

She felt her mouth drop open, and then swallowed rapidly.

'Get. . .get to you?' she squeaked.

She cleared her throat, opened her suddenly dry mouth to ask what on earth he meant, and snapped it shut at the gleam that had entered those molten black eyes.

His gaze drifted over her face, considered her carefully confined hair for a moment, and then eventually settled on her lips.

'There's something about you that. . .'

He paused, and then his voice deepened to a wondering murmur that sent a sudden flame straight through the region near Ellena's heart.

'First I thought you were a teenager. A very young one at that. Then I was sure you were just a very beautiful, but thoroughly exhausted, unhappy woman ready to burst into tears. I found myself wanting to comfort you. To hold you.'

Ellena couldn't take her fascinated gaze away from the puzzled eyes that lifted and seemed to search out her very soul.

A flash of amusement suddenly lightened the dark eyes again. The moustache twitched. Ellena braced herself.

'Then something about the commanding manner in which you ordered me away from the doorway made me suspect who you were. You had to be a matron!'

Heat flooded Ellena. She jumped up.

'My, my. You do blush red, don't you?' He was openly laughing at her now.

'I'm glad you're amused, Mr Nicoletti. Now, I have a great deal to catch up on and——'

'Ben.'

Ellena took a deep breath as she continued her fight for control. She refused to admit there was something about this man that frightened her. He was so sure of himself, and there was a depth to him that something deep inside her responded to. Her long-guarded immunity towards tall, dark and handsome men was under threat.

He stood up, still smiling at her.

She had always hated to be made to feel her size against men who were at least one hundred and eighty centimetres. They even gave her a kink in the neck. . .

But she suddenly realised he was just the ideal height for her. Her eyes were on a level with his lips. And that made her irrationally angry. Perhaps a little fearful. . .but definitely angry!

Then for once she allowed herself the luxury of letting that anger sweep through her in an unstoppable flood.

'*Mr* Nicoletti, you're a royal pain in the neck. You've done nothing but snarl at me, fling unjustified accusations at me, try to undermine my authority, upset an old lady's confidence I had just managed to bolster, and allow this whole place to be turned on its head! Chris must have been crazy to let you be the administrator!'

She didn't flinch even when all trace of his beautiful smile was wiped away. Nor when he took a step closer. She just raised her head. Her voice grew louder.

'Its obvious you know very little about the running of a place like this. How dare you speak to me the way you have? How dare you interfere with the staff levels of this place? I wouldn't be surprised if you insisted on the meal changes also and——'

A sudden gasp from the doorway swung both pairs of furious faces now closely confronting each other towards the person standing there. It was Linda Terry. Even through her fury, Ellena recognised the malicious delight that flashed across her face.

'Oh, dear! I'm sorry, Miss Provis. . . Ben. . . I——'

'Get out!' snarled Ellena. 'I'll ring you when I've finished here.'

'Oh, no, you don't!' Ben's voice now matched hers in its anger. 'Linda, get back in here!'

Ellena was momentarily speechless.

'How dare you——?'

'You've said that already too many times!' he suddenly roared. 'I dare, because, whether you like it or not, I am the administrator of Macallister's until the owners say otherwise. And never in my life before has an employee spoken to me the way you just have!'

They stared furiously at each other.

With horror, Ellena suddenly realised their voices must have been heard by the patients and any visitors now in the lounge room. Not to mention any staff near by!

Not giving an inch, she lowered her voice and hissed at him, 'Employee? For your information, you are not my boss. You have no direct authority over me. I alone am responsible for the nursing care given in this place. And for the nursing staff. I was employed by Dr Hansen and his wife the same way Matthew Long was, and it was made very clear to both of us that we each only answered to them, although we were expected to work in harmony together!'

There was a sudden arrested look on Ben's face. He looked across at Linda.

'That's not what you told me,' he said sharply.

'I. . .I didn't know. No one said. . .'

He continued to stare at her as she faltered and looked down, and then he looked back at Ellena. 'Nevertheless, until the owners return, and while I represent them, I *am* your "boss", as you put it.'

Ellena glared back at his dark face for a moment, and then turned abruptly and walked across to the window behind the desk. One hand came up to her quivering mouth as she fought for control.

For several moments there was a heavy silence behind her.

'Linda, would you be so kind as to go and get us all some coffee? I believe the three of us need to try and sort a few things out.'

Ben's voice was quiet but authoritative. Ellena felt vaguely relieved as she heard a faint rustle and realised the woman had disappeared without a word.

'Miss Provis?'

He had moved silently to stand beside her. Ellena continued to stare blindly out of the window.

'Ellena, look, I've given a lot of thought today to your reactions this morning, not to mention the other night.' He spoke rapidly, but very softly. 'I realised quite a few things just don't add up. The impression I've been given of you contradicts so much of what I'd heard of you from the Hansens and George Macallister during the last year. Not to mention reports in your file. . .and the patients. . .' He paused, and then an urgent note crept into his voice. 'I believe it's imperative that we try and clarify a few things with Linda Terry.'

Ellena felt her agitated breathing calm as his soft words flowed over her. But she was still bewildered and upset by her uncharacteristic outburst, especially when Linda Terry must have heard every word!

He waited a moment, and when she didn't stir, he reached out a hand and touched one of the African violets.

'I suddenly just found it very hard to believe that the woman I met that night who cares so passionately for these beautiful things could possibly be the fearful dragon I'd been told about.'

She turned abruptly and looked at him in amazement.

'Told about! Someone actually said that——?'

'I was as fast as I could,' Linda's breathless voice interrupted. 'Ann will bring us a tray so we can start our little talk straight away.'

They both swung around and looked at her.

Something in their expressions chased the smile from Linda's face. She hesitated momentarily, but then said importantly with a forced smile, 'I'm afraid I still have a lot to do before the afternoon staff can take over, so shall we sit down and——?'

'Of course,' Ellena interrupted with a steely note in her voice. 'Please take a seat, both of you. We are all too busy to waste any more time. And if it were not for the fact that you are off duty tomorrow, Sister Terry, we could have postponed this. . .' she paused and glared at Ben '. . .this talk until I've had a chance to orientate myself more to the situation here.'

No one, but no one, gave orders in her office!

She knew that Ben at least had grasped the fact that she was very firmly taking charge by the slight twitch of his moustache. For a moment she held her breath, wondering if he would insist on taking over, and was immensely relieved when he merely nodded and fetched the chair she indicated. He waited politely until they had both sat down before sitting himself.

Ellena pulled her notebook from her pocket. 'I had asked Sister Terry already to come to my office this afternoon because I noticed several areas this morning that need to be addressed immediately,' she began briskly, and was proud of the fact that her voice held hardly a tremor.

'In other words you noticed that this place had been

turned on its head, I think was the expression you used,' Ben snapped and then added as she opened her mouth, 'and I know that's why Linda's here.'

He stared directly back at her as she glanced up at him with surprise. His expression was unreadable. She could hardly believe those harsh words had come from the same man who a few moments ago. . .

Ben avoided her eyes and glanced quickly away to the other woman.

'I knew you intended to speak to Sister Terry. That's one reason I'm here. I rang just after lunch to see how things were and Linda told me you had. . .er. . . demanded to see her at the end of her shift.'

Looking uncomfortable, Linda said, 'You. . .you happened to ring just after she had. . .had told me——'

'"Screamed at you" was the way you put it, I believe,' Ben said in the same abrupt voice.

'I *screamed* at you!'

Ellena was dumbfounded and momentarily speechless at such a perversion of the truth. Then she opened her mouth again, only to snap it shut when Ben's sudden glance at Ellena was filled with a warning look, so quickly veiled, that for a moment she thought she must have imagined it.

'Sister Terry believed her dismissal was imminent. Isn't that so? And, as I'm responsible for any changes made, I thought it only fair to be here.'

'*You* are responsible for changes concerning the patients' welfare? But that's the prerogative of *nursing* admin! Why. . .?'

Ellena's voice had trailed off in sheer astonishment at this man's appalling ignorance of the structure of authority in a health care institution, and was still

staring at him, when, to her increasing consternation
and bewilderment, the woman burst into tears.

'She. . .she was awful! All morning she kept on at
me!' Linda's head was bowed as she sobbed loudly in
between her words. 'Nothing seemed to satisfy her! I
was so behind with my work after spending so much
time telling her about the patients. And. . .and then
she said if I wasn't in her office by three o'clock. . .'

Ellena started to protest, but was still again as Ben
shook his head slightly at her.

'So you begged me to rush to your rescue.' Ben's
voice was quite matter-of-fact.

Ellena stared in blank amazement at him and then
back at the woman crying copiously. When she looked
back at Ben he was watching her own reaction steadily,
completely ignoring the apparently distraught woman.
Ellena straightened her back further, tilted her chin
and stared back at him just as steadily.

A very slight twinkle of appreciation flashed into his
eyes. But then he frowned, holding her gaze as he
waited silently until the noisy sobs faded to a few
sniffles.

'Well, Miss Provis,' he said very slowly at last,
'apparently you after all do have the authority to hire
and fire staff. Is Sister Terry about to lose her
position here?'

Every instinct in Ellena wanted to say 'Yes!' but all
her warning antennae were well and truly on red alert.
There was something happening here that required
very cautious action.

CHAPTER FIVE

'I HAVE never asked anyone to resign, or sacked anyone without very strong reasons,' Ellena said very distinctly at last, not for one moment prepared to admit to them that she had never had cause to do either for any reasons at all! 'Do you think I have any cause to wish you not to be working for us here, Sister Terry?'

Ben nodded with approval, but the woman next to him was suddenly very still, her head still bent and her fingers clenched on her handkerchief.

'Well, Sister Terry?' Ben's voice was suddenly very cold.

'No, no, of course not.' Linda lifted her head at last and stared at them both defiantly. 'I've worked many long hours overtime the past four weeks which I've never claimed pay for. You. . .you. . .' she glared at Ellena '. . .you had seemed so pleasant and then you changed so unexpectedly, ordering me to your office the way you did!'

'The way I did, Sister Terry? And how exactly did I *order* you?' Ellena asked calmly.

'I. . .I. . .you. . .'

Ellena waited patiently until she faltered to a stop and looked swiftly away.

'I made a very simple request to see you in my office, in private, because I thought you would prefer no one else to hear what I had to say to you. You had for some reason, completely incomprehensible to me, incidentally, rostered yourself to work the weekend and

65

then have your two days off on my first days back at work. I also can't understand why the acting DON is even rostered to work shifts on the wards, considering her workload as well as your concern for the salary budget! There were still several things I would have appreciated you filling me in on before you left today, and a couple of things I wanted to say to you,' Ellena said curtly. 'I was only forced to make the request an *order* when you informed me you could not come to my office because you wished to leave early!'

Ben moved abruptly, and glanced at his watch. His voice was crisp and full of authority as he said, 'Right, the afternoon staff will be arriving any moment. Shall we get on with it? What else did you want to say?'

'I just said I thought Sister Terry would prefer me to speak to her privately,' Ellena snapped pointedly.

Linda opened her mouth, but Ben snarled suddenly, 'But you heard me just say that she wanted me to be here, so I'm staying.' He folded his arms, leaned back in his chair and suddenly smiled at the now obviously uncertain sister. 'Linda and I have worked very closely these past few weeks and I'm sure I can be of assistance to you both, Miss Provis.'

Ellena looked from one to the other suspiciously. Although that ridiculous moustache had twitched, and the lines on his face had tilted as he smiled, she noted that the smile had not reached his eyes. Suddenly she felt absurdly hurt that this man still did not trust her not to unfairly 'tear strips', as he had put it, off one of the staff.

Not just any member of the staff, she thought with a pang. Linda was a very attractive woman. Ellena suspected she was several years older than herself, perhaps about the same age as Ben. Her dark auburn hair and slim height would look wonderful beside this very masculine man.

Suddenly she wondered if they were friends away from work. How close did his 'close' really mean?

And then she felt a very unfamiliar stab of absurd jealousy for this woman she was about to reprimand.

'I knew I had taken enough of your time this morning, Sister, just doing the round of the patients,' Ellena forced herself at last to say very professionally and stalling for time, 'and I didn't like to take any more of your time to ask you about the new admissions expected tomorrow. I couldn't find any information written down anywhere about them.'

'I left that info with Ben,' Linda said sharply.

'Yes, that's no problem at all,' Ben added quickly, 'I had already planned to be here in plenty of time to deal with them.'

'*You* deal with new admissions?' Ellena asked with surprise.

He frowned. 'I believe I'm quite capable of looking after new admissions.'

'And were you going to decide which beds they were to occupy, and sort out their medical needs also?'

His expression darkened further. 'No, the sister in charge does that.'

'And does the sister on duty in the morning know whether the patient requires a right-side or left-side access to a bed depending on any mobility problem; in fact, even if the patient is male or female? And has she made sure Dr Gill knows about them so he can admit them and do all the paperwork required for ongoing care?'

There was silence. Ben stared at Ellena thoughtfully, and then turned to Linda. 'Linda?'

She looked sullenly back at him. 'That's all sorted out when they arrive!' she snapped.

'No, that will not be sorted out when they arrive,' Ellena said sharply. 'No patient coming to Macallister's while I have been in charge has had to wait in the lounge-room and made to feel unwanted while staff move other patients around to accommodate them. Most of the old dears have already spent weeks in hospitals and are upset about the move anyway. Usually patients arrive here very apprehensive, to say the least. Most are plain scared! And I have always insisted they are made to feel special. Very special! And that includes adequate preparation for their arrival! The mornings are always very busy as it is, and the staff on this afternoon should make sure everything is ready anyway.'

She looked steadily from one to the other and waited.

'The new admissions are both male,' Linda said at last, just a little too loudly.

'Diagnosis?' snapped Ellena.

'Er. . .er. . .I'm not really sure. . . I. . .'

'Referring doctors?'

It was Ben who told her, and then he added shortly, 'I also believe one gentleman has Parkinson's disease; he's an old patient of Dr Hansen's. And Linda, I thought you said you'd been told the other patient has a neurological disorder which is causing his mobility to be severely affected.'

Ellena noticed a strange expression cross Linda's face before it was hidden as she swung round to Ben and said brightly, 'Did I say that?' Then she shrugged and turned back to Ellena. 'It was one of those mad-house days and I'm afraid I've no clear recollection of it all.'

Ellena glanced at Ben's creased forehead before making a couple of notes. 'Do you know their ages?'

'No, of course not!' Linda's voice was scornful.

Ellena slowly lifted her head and looked at her enquiringly. 'You don't think it will matter if a young sixty-year-old shares a room with a ninety-year-old? That two men of a similar background and age would not enjoy each other's company a lot more than two completely incompatible gentlemen?'

There was silence. Linda bit her lip and tossed her head.

'Do you know where they are coming from? Home or hospital?'

Silence again.

'Do you know if their next of kin or significant other will be with them?'

Silence.

'Have they been informed of what they will need here? For example, that they dress in their comfortable clothes every day, and do not stay in pyjamas? Have they been asked to make sure all their things are marked with their names? Will they be bringing in their current prescribed medications with them?'

Ellena snapped off the questions, waited a telling moment, and then sighed.

'There is really no excuse for these things not being done. The protocol for all new admissions is clearly written in the protocol folder.'

'The what folder?'

Ellena looked at Ben sharply. She could have sworn there had been amusement in his voice, but he stared gravely back at her. Abruptly she stood up. As she walked over to a cupboard and pulled out a large ring-back folder, her legs began to tremble. Hoping desperately they would not notice the tremor in her hand, she placed the folder on her desk.

'That contains the protocol for the Macallister Rehabilitation Complex,' she said briefly. 'There is also a copy at the nurses' station. *All* new staff are automatically informed that their first responsibility is to become familiar with everything in it. It also contains the roles of the administrative staff.'

Ben's hand shot out and picked it up. 'Well, I for one haven't seen this before. But then, I didn't get the normal chance to talk to my predecessor. You've studied this, of course, Linda?' he added conversationally.

'Of course,' Linda said rapidly, 'but you know how busy we've been, and there has been so much to learn while I filled in as DON. And without a deputy too,' she added significantly. 'No doubt there are some things I've missed.'

'Like the fact that all patients, unless too ill, are to have their breakfast in the dining-room?' Ellena asked very softly.

Ben looked up at her suddenly, but she kept her intent gaze on Linda. Colour rushed into the other woman's face.

'The most ridiculous, stupid idea ever,' Linda snapped angrily. 'It takes far too much time for the staff to take forty people to a dining-room and then afterwards have to take them back to the lounge-room or all the way back to the bathrooms for their showers. Whoever thought that one up certainly had not much idea of time management—or economical management! And when I pointed it out to Ben, he ordered the change. And I was right. We've been able to cut right back on the staff needed since,' she added proudly. 'And Ben was very happy not to have such a large salary bill.'

'Oh, I'm sure he was happy,' Ellena said quickly, the dark side of her nature beginning to rather enjoy itself. 'I'm just not quite so sure that Dr Hansen and his wife will appreciate your changing their carefully thought-out routine! Or the staff levels they worked out with me,' she added significantly.

There was silence as the two opposite stared at her. Linda bit her lip, her colour fading.

'Chris and Jean wrote this protocol?' Ben's voice was very quiet.

Ellena looked back at him, suddenly a little ashamed of her nastiness. 'Well, they've kindly changed some of it after considering some of my suggestions since we opened. Theory doesn't always work out exactly as expected when put into practice.'

'But you don't think they will approve of the changes we've made?'

'No,' she said bluntly. 'They were very insistent that the patients need as much opportunity and motivation to be mobilised as possible. Going to a meal has more purpose than just being taken for a walk just anywhere.' Her tone hardened. 'Besides, it may be far more economical for the nurses' wage bill, but I strongly suspect not for the kitchen and domestic staff wage bill. I take it you've had to advertise for more staff for that area already?'

To her satisfaction, Ben nodded, grim-faced.

'They should have had more staff well before this,' Ellena continued firmly. 'It takes up a lot more time making up individual trays, delivering them, and then collecting them again. I see you had to buy more trays and that large trolley. Besides all that, if you read the domestic staff's protocol, you would know that no cleaning is permitted in rooms when food is being consumed, so the whole cleaning schedule is now out of kilter as well.'

There was silence as Ellena looked from one to the other.

'It's still much easier for the nurses anyway,' Linda said defensively at last. 'And after all, the nurses are the ones whose best interests are the primary responsibility of the DON, aren't they?'

There was a pause.

Ellena began to feel a little sorry for the woman. It was becoming more and more obvious that she had been way out of her depth as acting DON. She swallowed back the words she had been about to say.

From her very first days as a terrified student nurse, it had been drilled into her repeatedly by their old tutor sister that the patient was the most important person in any medical facility. Sadly, that focus had often appeared to have shifted in the minds of many professionals in recent years. And certainly in this woman's.

One of the reasons she had been delighted to be able to work for the Hansens had been because they had been very strong on that very point. It had been very clearly spelt out that her primary role was to provide excellent care of the patients. And certainly, that did include looking after the nurses and making sure they were happy in their work, but the patients' needs were still top priority.

'The DON's responsibility here extends to all indoor

staff responsible for care of the patient,' Ellena mur-mured at last. 'I believe you are still doing your administration certificate, Sister Terry?' she asked quite gently.

'That's right, but I've only another few weeks to go.' Linda glanced at her watch, and then stood up. 'I really must go. The reports——'

'Sit down, Sister.'

Ellena's voice was still quiet, and Linda opened her mouth, but then saw the expression on her DON's face. She sank back. Her face lost some of its colour.

'First of all, do you still mind Mr Nicoletti hearing what I have to say next?'

'*I'm* very interested in anything else you have to say, Miss Provis.' Ben's voice was hard. 'In fact, I insist on staying.'

'Very well, then,' Ellena said briskly. 'First of all, Sister Terry, I believe you told Julie Newton that I had refused point-blank to cut short my holidays. Why?'

What seemed to be genuine amazement filled the sister's face. 'Why? Because she asked me why you weren't back.'

'But why on earth did you say I had refused when I knew nothing about what had happened until this morning?'

'Because Dr Hansen had given Sister Terry that information to pass on to me!' Ben's deep voice growled. 'I don't think he intended that information to be broadcast to all and sundry, though,' he added with a glare at Sister Terry.

'*Chris* told you! But how. . .?'

Ellena felt even more confused. There was no reason for Linda to be lying, but why on earth would Chris pass on something so untrue?

'Look, surely the ins and outs of all that can be sorted out when the Hansens return,' Ben said impatiently. 'If that's all, perhaps Linda can get back to the wards now.'

Ellena straightened and glared at him. 'No, that's by no means all! When you return from your days off, Sister Terry, certain changes will have been implemented. You may not agree with them, or even approve of them. But I expect your full co-operation.'

'Naturally, Ellena,' snapped Linda.

'And that's another thing. Although we do encourage the use of first names of staff by patients, I would really prefer you to call me Miss Provis, especially in front of patients and visitors.'

'Yes, I believe I agree with that,' Ellena was surprised to hear Ben say thoughtfully. 'In my experience,' he added, 'it does tend to help establish one's authority. But what changes are you talking about? I haven't approved any changes.'

Ellena closed her eyes briefly. Here it was again. Ignorance of the DON's authority.

'They are changes *I* have the authority to make,' she snapped.

His eyes narrowed, but she was thankful when he refrained from speaking again.

Ellena looked blindly down at her notebook, dreading what else she knew she had to say. She had always hated reprimanding a member of staff. Quite unexpectedly, she felt a sense of relief that Ben had refused to leave them alone.

Deliberately avoiding Ben's watchful eyes, Ellena took a deep breath and stood up. She didn't realise she was every inch the matron he had teased her about as she looked steadily at Linda, who was still defiantly glaring at her.

'Your attitude, which I observed this morning towards staff and patients, I found completely unacceptable.'

Linda gasped, but Ellena continued in an inflexible voice.

'If I ever hear you using coarse language such as you did this morning, or if I ever hear you yelling at staff as you did today, I will be forced to take very serious disciplinary action. There is a code of conduct for registered nurses included in the Macallister Rehab Complex staff manual. Written again by the Hansens. I expect you to familiarise yourself with it. No further serious breaches will be tolerated.'

Linda began to splutter, but was silent again when Ellena held up a hand commandingly.

'I haven't finished yet. Your knowledge of the patients you were responsible for today was appalling. With the excellent references you have, I find that difficult to understand, even though I realise you've been too busy on the administration side to have time to catch up on everything to do with them. But you also worked on the ward yesterday. There were several very basic things you did not know this morning. For example, you couldn't even remember Mr Harrington's name and you've certainly spent some time with him before!'

Ellena took a deep breath, deciding it might be wiser not to mention that particular slip-up of Linda's any more at this point.

'Knowing the names of our patients is a very important part of seeing them as individuals in our care,' she continued evenly, 'not as merely "that CVA" or "that double amputee"! In an acute hospital ward with a constant changeover of patients, it may be excusable. I personally doubt it. Here, where our patients are long-term, there is no excuse whatsoever.'

Linda stood up shakily.

Ellena continued sharply. 'Your knowledge of basic rehabilitation techniques is also appalling. Perhaps that can be explained by the fact that you've mainly nursed in other specialised acute care areas. I noticed in your résumé that you have only worked with geriatric patients in nursing homes. This is, most definitely, different nursing from what you would have experienced there. Our aim here is to try and keep our patients from having to go to nursing homes! I will arrange a time for you to see me after your days off, and I will personally go through several things with you.'

She glanced at her watch. 'I apologise if you believe I unfairly took up too much of your time today. When you've finished all your work you may go. Don't worry about handing over to the afternoon staff, I'll see to that myself.'

White-faced and subdued at last, Linda turned to leave.

'Just a moment, Linda!' Ben was frowning at Ellena. 'Despite what Miss Provis has just said, I want to assure you that I personally appreciate the way you stepped in and helped out when this establishment found itself without any nursing personnel in administration, and——'

Ellena heard the scathing criticism in his voice, and interrupted him abruptly, saying as steadily as she could, 'I have no doubt you have done the best you could these past few weeks. Mr Nicoletti has already expressed to me his appreciation for the way you stepped in and so willingly helped out. It is because

of that alone that I'm prepared to overlook other things
that have happened today.'

She paused. Linda flashed her a look so full of hatred
and vindictiveness that Ellena grasped the desk with
both hands.

'You may go,' she somehow managed to say steadily.

Then Ben and Ellena were alone.

Ellena fumbled to her chair, and sat down. She
started to tremble visibly. It was all too soon after the
last few traumatic weeks. She was vaguely aware that
Ben moved. She heard the door close and a few
moments later she raised her head as a glass was thrust
into her hand.

'Phew! That was some speech,' she heard Ben say.

Her trembling increased. Some water spilt on to the
desk. Then a large, warm hand took the glass from
her and held it to her lips.

'Drink it,' he ordered curtly.

She swallowed a couple of mouthfuls, only then
realising how dry her throat felt.

'What on earth's happened to that coffee I
requested?' he snapped and strode towards the door
just as someone knocked on it.

Ellena sat still as he spoke abruptly and then took
a tray holding three steaming cups from the flustered
young nurse. He placed the tray on her desk and thrust
a cup at her. Gratefully her chilled fingers closed on
its warmth. He took his own cup over to the window,
and she was suddenly grateful for his sensitivity in
giving her time to recover.

They were both quiet for some time. Then he stirred,
and came back to his chair.

'She hates you,' he said suddenly.

She raised strained eyes and let him see the

devastation that knowledge had been to her. There had been rejection in the past even from people she had loved, but never with such hostility. And never from a stranger.

'I know,' she said harshly. 'No one has ever looked at me quite like that before. Not even Howard. . .' She bit her lip, and then added sadly, 'And what's even worse, I don't have the faintest idea why.'

His face had shown momentary curiosity at her mention of Howard's name, but then he actually snorted. 'It would be easy to think it was merely because of the reprimand you just handed out. But the way I've heard her speak of you in the past when she'd never even met you. . .I wonder. . .'

He stared down at the cup in his hand for several moments while Ellena watched him, her own thoughts beginning to race.

She had encountered plenty of professional jealousy in the past, also personality conflicts. But still. . .

'Sister Terry has tremendous qualifications. Far more than I have. She——'

'She certainly has plenty of pieces of paper that say she has completed many different areas of training,' Ben interrupted. 'Obstetrics, theatre certificates, intensive care certificate, geriatrics, coronary care. . .'

Ellena shuddered.

He paused, and then said, 'But did you notice in her nursing record book that she hasn't worked at the same place for more than a few weeks for the last couple of years? And all those excellent referrals are more than two years old?'

Ellena dragged her thoughts back from the coronary care unit she had so recently spent agonising time in, not as a nurse but a frantic relative, to find he was studying her thoughtfully.

'That could have been for many reasons,' Ellena said quickly, 'and I'm sure Julie would have checked her references.'

'Just the same, it may pay to make more enquiries. Ellena, there's one more thing you should know. Linda mentioned casually once that the local nurses' union rep is one of her best friends. I don't know how true that is, but be careful, huh?'

She looked at him with dawning comprehension of those warning glances. The local area nurses' association was known for being militant. Before she could speak, he suddenly put his cup back on the tray decisively and stood up.

'There's really no more time for us to talk about this. What if we postpone it to another day?'

He glanced at his watch, and then so did Ellena.

She groaned. 'There's just so much to do, and now I've stupidly let that woman go so I have to hand over.'

'Anything I can do?'

She looked at him, suddenly comforted and warmed by his quiet strength. As she stood up she smiled at him, and saw his expression change again. A flame flickered deep in his eyes and that now familiar flash of an electric current shooting in response through her own body was almost expected.

Confused, she made a pretence of consulting her notepad, hoping he would think the trembling starting up in her hands again was still caused by the confrontation with Linda. 'I think I might take you up on that,' she began to say as briskly as she could. 'The first thing is to try and get more staff to work tomorrow.'

She hadn't realised he had moved closer until a finger touched under her chin and lifted her face towards him.

'You have a very beautiful smile. It turns those large hazel eyes of yours almost green. I wish you would smile more often, though.'

His own incredibly dark eyes were glowing with masculine appreciation and warmth.

Then Ellena felt the heat of his gaze increase as he saw her confusion, and the sudden wonder she was feeling that this man's touch, this virtual stranger, could make her feel things she had thought lost to her so many years before.

'I'm really sorry I've been so ignorant of so many things and let this place get in the mess you claim it is. There have been huge problems as well with builders and architects on the units that have taken far too much of my time.'

Two apologies in an hour! she thought as she stared speechlessly at him. Only a man very sure of himself, a strong man, could afford to admit to being in the wrong so freely.

'I wish I knew what it is about you. . .' she heard him mutter her own thoughts out loud.

Before she could move, his face came closer, and in a daze she felt the tickle of his moustache and then the warmth of his soft lips. It started out as a very gentle kiss of consolation, but she felt her own lips move, and then his hardened.

Dimly she was aware that his fingers left her face. A strong arm slipped to her waist and drew her closer as the kiss deepened. It was when she felt her own mouth respond helplessly and the tip of his tongue slide around and over her lips that she tensed. Abruptly his arms fell away and he stepped back.

They stared at each other.

His eyes were dazed, reflecting her own feelings. Then they changed, and she saw a mixture of consternation and anger.

'I'm. . .I'm. . .' she began wildly to apologise as a feeling of absolute shame swept through her. It had been her reaction that had changed the kiss to something she now wasn't sure how to handle.

Surely she was mature enough, had learnt many hard lessons about hormones and emotions not to have yielded to the sheer beauty and magnetism of this. . . this man who, even as she stared at him with increasing horror, drew himself up to his full height.

'That should never have happened!' he condemned in a harsh voice. He turned towards the door, and tossed over his shoulder, 'I'll get the folder with the current information on casuals for you. You'd better pay a visit to the kitchen staff before they change shifts and before you go and meet the other nurses now arriving.'

Handing out orders again, she fumed.

'Just. . .just a moment!' she managed as she desperately pulled herself together. 'I really do need all the information you have on the new admissions.'

She was proud of the snap that sounded in her voice.

He stopped and swung around. They stared at each other across the room. Unexpectedly his eyes started to twinkle, and she felt her own heart lighten with sheer relief as he suddenly grinned.

'Will do, Matron!'

Ellena thought of a few grey-haired, grim-faced matrons she had known over the years. How often had a matron been kissed before in her own office by

someone she had only met briefly a few days before
for the first time? And how many times had a matron
kissed a handsome man right back?

Her sense of humour surfaced for the first time for
many long dreary days and even weeks. Ellena found
herself actually starting to chuckle.

'For goodness' sake! Don't go calling me that in
front of anyone! The older generation get confused
enough with all the changes in nursing without you
confusing them further just after they've got used to
calling me Miss Provis or even Ellena!'

His surprised gleam of admiration quickly became
a full-bellied laugh that sent tingles right through her
in response.

Then he turned away, still smiling broadly, and continued on his way.

CHAPTER SIX

A BEAMING smile of relief was still on Ellena's own face as she left the admin area and entered the lounge-room, but any lingering feeling of euphoria quickly disappeared as there was a sudden lull in the murmur of voices in the room.

Oh, no! she groaned silently. Sunday afternoon visitors! And no doubt most of them had heard the row in the office. Including that last burst of merriment. Thank goodness no one could have seen what else had happened!

She felt a wave of scarlet flood her face, forced herself to nod briefly and then put on her cool professional smile as several curious pairs of eyes were focused on her. Without pausing she hastened her stride and thankfully escaped into the dining-room quickly before anyone could stop her.

To her relief she was told by the person in charge that the head cook would be on duty first thing in the morning. She had got on very well with him when he had been employed to set up the catering facilities. But she wasn't quite prepared for the tremendous relief that lit up the weekend cook's face when she asked her to leave a message for him that she would like breakfast served in the dining-room in the morning if it wasn't too inconvenient.

'There!' Mavis beamed. 'What do you know? He swore blind you'd sort this place out again if you came back. Of course he won't mind. He'll be only too happy.' A hint of worry flickered. 'Will. . .will that be a permanent change, Miss Provis? For weekends as well?'

When Ellena nodded quickly, she sighed with relief and confided, 'It's been so worrying not knowing what to prepare so that the poor old dears can manage if the nurses are too busy to help them.'

Ellena managed not to say what she thought about that! And eventually escaped after Mavis had insisted on introducing her to one of her helpers who had only commenced work that weekend.

It wasn't until much later that night as she was reviewing the day and almost asleep that she remembered that Mavis had said 'if'. 'If' she returned? Where had that idea come from? She pondered briefly about it before succumbing to the exhaustion that overwhelmed her.

But she never gave a thought to it then as she hurried towards the wards, her mind churning with all that was to be done.

Familiar faces looked up at the DON with varying expressions of relief and apprehension as she hurried up to the nurses' station. She was very relieved to see that the RN coming on duty was Joan Wheat, a very sensible, experienced woman.

There was a chorus of subdued greetings which she returned with a smile, managing to answer briefly the inevitable questions about her 'holidays'. To her heart-felt relief, Linda Terry was nowhere in sight. But neither were the other nurses who had been working all day.

'I wonder if someone would mind asking Ann and Maureen if they could join us as soon as possible? The day-shift nurse can come and get them if she requires any assistance for a few minutes.'

When one of them had rushed off, she said, 'Now, I haven't had a chance to absorb who's doing which shift tomorrow, but are any of you doing a quick shift by any chance?'

With relief, Ellena saw the RN nod grimly. She grimaced at her sympathetically, knowing how all nurses hated working a late shift until eleven followed by a seven start the next morning, especially if they lived any distance away. She and Julie had done their utmost to eliminate them from the roster, but an occasional one was still unavoidable.

'In fact I've got three quick shifts this next fortnight,' Sister Wheat said shortly.

Ellena nearly groaned out loud. Another thing to do. Check the roster for the next fortnight that commenced the next day.

She pushed that thought away as the other nurses returned.

'Miss. . .Miss Provis. Sister Terry's gone off duty,' Ann White said breathlessly. 'She was really raging! She——'

'That's all right, Ann,' Ellena interrupted swiftly, 'I know all about it, and she had my permission to leave. Now, we are already running late. I must confess I'm glad most of you are working tomorrow as there will be several changes I can fill you in on now.'

She told them quickly about the change back to having all patients out of bed for breakfast. It was met with varying responses. A couple frowned, including the RN.

'As soon as we've had the report, I'm going to be ringing up and getting casuals to come in and help, including at least one RN. Only the night shift is not

woefully understaffed. And I'll be in early myself,'
Ellena added rapidly.

The frowns disappeared. 'Thank heavens for that!'
Sister Wheat exclaimed fervently.

'Now,' beamed Ellena, 'I told Sister Terry I'd take
the report.' She pulled a face. 'But somehow I think
it will be a case of you filling me in as we go through
the charts. And that's another thing. Please ask the
night staff to return all bed charts to the front of these
in the trolley. Now, would anyone like to grab a cup
of coffee to drink as we go as this may take some
time? And if necessary, I can stay and help you catch
up a bit afterwards.'

The staff relaxed completely as they discussed the
patients. But it very quickly became blatantly obvious
to Ellena that most of the nurses, especially the RNs
in charge of shifts, had become frustrated innumerable
times when they had tried to continue rehabilitation
of patients as the hours of the staff had been cut back.
Other directives and initiatives had also been hindered.

'Sister Terry just wouldn't listen to anyone!' one of
the ENs, Alison Pleasant, burst out indignantly when
Ellena asked about Mr Harrington. 'She insisted Sister
wait for the physio to show us how to start him
correctly. Even I could have done that!' she added
disgustedly.

When they reached Mrs Brown, Ellena was very
surprised to discover that she had not been thoroughly
examined and investigated yet by James Gill.

'He's had to rush through his rounds lately,' the RN
said grimly. 'Pressure of work was the excuse.'

One of the ENs giggled, but was quelled by a glare
from Maureen Smythe. Ellena raised her eyebrows at
them and they both subsided with a stain of red rising

in their cheeks. There was some gossip there about Dr Gill, she surmised, and decided to ignore it for the moment.

Ellena turned back to the RN, who looked a little flustered.

'He. . .er. . .always needed to get away in a rush. Sister Terry was with him. He said just to do the ordinary observations,' she said rapidly. 'I was on duty the evening after her admission, so I commenced the usual fourth-hourly TPR and daily lying and standing BP for the usual three days like we always did after admission for someone like her straight from home who's been having falls.' She paused, and took a deep breath before continuing angrily, 'When I came back on duty the next day I got a blast from Sister Terry for wasting everyone's time!'

'And no patients have had even weekly routine lying and standing BP obs, or weighs, for three weeks!' Maureen chipped in again.

'I tried to explain to her about the effect of some drugs on elderly people causing postural hypotension, the need to know fluid retention and help diet control by weighing—even about low BPs causing dizziness and falls. But——' Joan cut herself off abruptly.

'Right!' said Ellena after a moment. 'You all know the strife we'd be in if Dr Hansen did a round tomorrow and we didn't have this basic info for him! Do as many BPs as you can find time for tonight, and tell the night and morning shifts the same. Get them all done as soon as possible. We'll weigh everyone again, as we used to, next weekend. And now, there's only Mrs Davis to go.'

There was a momentary stillness. Ellena had already guessed what must have happened, but she tensed.

The moment was broken by the sound of rapid footsteps approaching. Their heads swung around as Ben Nicoletti appeared.

The chorus of enthusiastic greetings covered the DON's sudden confusion and swiftly indrawn breath, which she only released as he included her in his smile and friendly, 'Hi, everyone!'

Several eyes swung suddenly from his face back to hers and she knew that they had heard about their loud fight.

'Afraid I have to race away, Mat. . .Miss Provis,' he said smoothly as the flash in her eyes dared him to call her Matron again.

That wretched moustache moved. She vividly remembered how it had felt. Like silk. Pressed against her face as his lips had. . .

Suddenly the DON's mantel of being in control deserted her for the second time that day.

'I. . .er. . .I'm sorry about that. . .' she heard her voice say huskily.

She cleared her throat and saw his eyes blaze at her. And then realised what she had said. She wished desperately she could curl up and quietly vanish as startled expressions appeared on the nurses' faces. Eyes stared at her in wonder, and then stared harder as she felt her face flame.

'I. . .I. . .er. . .mean——'

Her stutter was interrupted by his sudden bellow of laughter. 'I can't tell you how glad I am that you're sorry I'm leaving. But I'm afraid I must get back to a special family party, a wedding anniversary.' Mischief blazed at her discomfiture, and then he handed her a couple of sheets of paper. 'All the info I have about the new admissions.'

'Th-thank you,' she managed stiffly.

'And I've left the folder on casual staff on your desk. I'm not sure how up to date it is.' With a wave, he turned and was gone as quickly as he had arrived.

There was silence as nobody moved. Ellena was sure she had never felt so embarrassed before in her life as she stared blindly down at the papers he had given her. Then she was shocked to realise how utterly miserable she also felt at the thought of Ben daring to kiss her on his own wedding anniversary.

'It must be Mr Nicoletti's parents' fortieth anniversary, which he mentioned last week,' Joan Wheat's voice said quietly. 'Now, I believe we were up to Mrs Davis.'

Ellena felt a rush of sheer relief and then gratitude towards the older woman as she kept her eyes down and picked up the chart in front of her again. When she was sure she had control of her voice she lifted her head and looked steadily back at the RN. To her relief there was only a hint of sympathy in her eyes. Then that disappeared as Joan frowned.

'Her family are hopeless!' she said.

For one wild moment, Ellena thought she must mean Ben's family, and then pulled herself together.

'Mrs Davis's daughter, who lives in Newcastle, obviously feels guilty that her husband keeps insisting there's no way she could cope with looking after her mother in their own home,' Joan continued. 'The brother who lives in Sydney is at loggerheads with them all and just said it was ridiculous for his mother to even consider going home by herself again. He has all the reasons down pat why his wife couldn't be expected to have her live with them—one reason of

course being this increasing nocturnal incontinence.
After his last visit, Mrs Davis was very down. As well
as that. . .' She paused, obviously wondering how to
word her next statement.

'As well as that, Sister Terry put her spoke in,' said
Maureen Smythe bluntly.

The RN began to protest, but than she caught
Ellena's eye and stopped.

'Mrs Davis tells me she hasn't been able to get
enough sleep,' Ellena said calmly. 'I don't see anywhere in here that she was ever put on a sleep chart,
even before she was commenced on Serepax. Would
you please start one immediately? Not just night staff,
but a twenty-four-hour one, please. I know she's been
assessed by the government geriatric assessment team
for nursing home care, but I still want you to encourage
her to do as much as she can for herself again. Do
everything you can to build up her self-esteem. Most
of you should know by now that we just don't give up
this easily on one of our patients,' she added grimly,
and was pleased to see a few nods of agreement and
renewed purpose.

Ellena left it at that for the time being, making a note
in her book to talk to James Gill about the oxazepam
sedative he had ordered for Mrs Davis, as well as
perhaps starting her on a small dosage of amitriptyline.
Chris had prescribed it several times for other patients
with considerable success for their mild depression as
well as nocturnal enuresis.

'Now, is there anything else?' Ellena glanced at her
watch. 'Oh, the new admissions. Perhaps Sister Wheat
and I can sort that out and the rest of you had better
get on with your work.'

*   *   *

The next morning went remarkably smoothly, despite a few grumbles from patients who would much rather have stayed in bed until later. And despite the unexpected difficulty she had found in getting the extra staff.

The list of casual staff had appeared to be almost the same, and with a sigh she had picked up the phone to start the tedious task of trying to get people to work at short notice for the next day as well as the rest of the fortnight's roster.

But it had taken much longer than she had anticipated.

A couple of nurses had expressed astonishment to hear from her as they had apparently rung up during the past weeks to say they had full-time jobs and were no longer available. So that list of casuals was just one more thing that had not been kept up to date. And this one irritated her. Surely it would have only taken a couple of moments to cross their names off the list!

Then to her utter dismay, a total of three other nurses had said quite rudely they no longer wished to work where they were treated like dirt and expected to kill themselves with hard work! They had actually hung up on her before she could explain.

But eventually she had managed to get the extra staff booked to come in for most shifts to bring up the number of hours to an acceptable level. But she knew the casual penalty rates would blow the salary budget right out for the next fortnight, and wondered grimly what the new administrator would have to say to that.

A little to Ellena's surprise, but much to her relief, there was no sign of Ben Nicoletti until nine o'clock that morning. She had only been back in her own office a short while after spending the past two hours working side by side with the staff, when he arrived with the secretary.

She heard them laughing as they went past her door to the general office. A few minutes later, there was a quick knock on her door before it opened and Ben popped his head around.

'Morning, Miss Provis. Things go well this morning?'

When she nodded briefly, he merely said, 'Good,' cheerfully and disappeared.

She glowered at the closed door.

The least he could have done was show a bit more interest!

Only then did she realise how much she had been waiting and listening for him all through the hectic morning.

And he had called her Miss Provis.

When she had returned to her office the previous afternoon, it had seemed strangely lonely without his dark figure waiting for her. She had stood there in the empty room acknowledging the wonder of that kiss. For a moment she had felt again the pain of his rejection, but then her spirits had risen as she remembered their sudden shared sense of the ridiculous.

She had tried to push it all aside as she concentrated on the work she still had to get through before she could leave. But his face had kept on intruding, even after she had been tucked up very late in her bed just before she had fallen into an exhausted sleep. Even her dreams had been invaded by a tall, dark man who kept shouting at her until she'd woken up to find her bedclothes in a tangled mess around her and the alarm shrilling its unforgiving summons.

Now she deliberately pushed those wayward thoughts aside and picked up the notes about the new admissions and frowned at them again. The information was far too little. Not even a phone number to ring or a note to say where they were coming from so she could have checked them out.

She scowled at one of the notes. It had been scribbled in almost indecipherable handwriting on a scrap of notepaper. There was only the name, diagnosis and referring doctor. Ruefully she remembered that this particular doctor was noted for his fussiness in following correct procedure and doing meticulous rounds to see his patients were getting more than their share of care.

Then she frowned. In fact it wasn't at all like him to only send that bare information. He would have previously referred his patient to Chris, or his registrar, who would usually have seen the patient, and then he always sent very comprehensive, up-to-date history notes beforehand to be there before his patient arrived. Unless he had rung up James or Chris instead?

Ellena became more disgruntled during the next hour when she neither saw nor heard anything more of Ben. Once the fleeting thought crossed her mind that he might be intending to avoid her. Pushing the trace of hurt at that thought swiftly aside, she immersed herself in starting to fill out some of the endless reports required by endless government departments, many of which were already very late.

The first new admission arrived just as the patients were finishing their morning tea. Ellena was talking with the diversional therapist about using the leaves from the Africa violets for patients to try and strike in pots when she saw a thin, pale old gentleman being helped slowly through the front door by a much shorter, equally elderly lady. She was struggling also to manoeuvre a battered-looking old suitcase through the doorway at the same time.

They greeted Ellena with serious faces as she hurried forward to relieve the woman of the case.

'Hello, you must be Mr and Mrs Dredge. Welcome to Macallister's. I'm Ellena Provis, the director of nursing.' She smiled at them.

'Our. . .our daughter-in-law is just parking her car,' the rather stout lady said nervously.

'Well, why don't you both take a seat here in the foyer and wait for her?' Ellena said gently. 'When she arrives, we can go into my office for a chat and then you can all go and see your bedroom and have a look around.'

She watched as the old man tottered, his body rigid in a typical Parkinson's disease stance, his feet catching for a few moments, unable to move.

'Come on, love,' his wife said bracingly, 'just a few more steps.'

She held his arm, and spoke quietly to him again, but it took another few frustrating moments before he was at last shakily able to lift his feet and shuffle the few steps to the sensibly styled lounge chair for elderly people who found it difficult to get in and out of most very soft modern day chairs.

After they were seated, his frail hands shook quite violently until one of his wife's plump hands held them steadily.

'It. . .it's been rather upsetting for him this morning,' she said appealingly to Ellena with a worried look. 'He's not always as shaky as this.'

'I know, my dears,' Ellena said with her lovely sympathetic smile, 'but I'm sure you'll soon feel at home here.'

Two faded pairs of eyes were studying her so anxiously that her heart went out to them.

'And I know for sure that Dr Hansen would never have suggested that you come to us unless he was sure we could help you, sir.'

A look of relief gradually lightened the woman's lined face. Even Mr Dredge's face changed, his eyes brightening.

'There you are, John, love. Miss. . .Miss Provis will look after us! Jean said she would. And her so nice and pretty too! Why, you mightn't even want to come home too soon in a few days!'

As Ellena registered that they must know the Hansens personally, Mrs Dredge dug her elbow into her spouse's ribs. A faint smile twitched the pale lips on the old man's face.

'Always one to appreciate a pretty young woman, John is,' his wife teased him, and then looked up and all trace of amusement vanished as she looked towards the entrance.

The woman who entered was everything that Ellena had always wished she could be. She was strikingly beautiful, very tall with a very curvaceous figure more than adequately displayed by the latest expensive fashion in two-piece suits, and stalked towards them on very high-heeled shoes that perfectly matched the cream leather bag clutched in her hand. She could have come straight from a beauty salon, so perfect was every dark blonde hair and inch of make-up.

Ellena took a deep breath, but before she could speak, the woman ignored her completely and scowled at the elderly couple sitting down.

'What are you doing just sitting there?' she snapped

impatiently. 'I haven't got all day to waste waiting to take you back home, Mother.'

Ellena's eyes narrowed, and any nurse who knew her well would have immediately known it was wise to make herself scarce.

'They are sitting there waiting for their daughter-in-law,' she said quietly. 'I'm Miss Provis, the director of nursing of the Macallister Rehabilitation Complex. And your name would be. . .?'

She inclined her head autocratically, very much regretting her lack of inches as the woman stared down at her.

'I'm Annabel Burgess,' she said haughtily, and waited.

Ellena looked steadily back, aware that she was supposed to recognise the name. 'If you would take a seat, Mrs Burgess?'

'Miss! I use my maiden name professionally.'

Ellena deliberately kept her expression blank and merely said dismissively, 'I don't believe there is really any need for you to stay, *Miss* Burgess, if you are in a rush. It would be best for Mrs Dredge to stay as long as she can to help her husband settle in. I'm sure we'll be able to make arrangements to see that she gets home safely.'

She turned and smiled down at the two elderly people. Even if I have to take you home myself! she thought furiously as the return of the anxiety to their expressions made her ire rise even further.

'I'll just go and get my paperwork, and we'll take some notes out here to save you having to walk any further, Mr Dredge.'

Completely ignoring the now furious face on the elegant woman, she turned and hurried towards her office. At her door she hesitated, and then a rather naughty thought struck her.

She moved and knocked briefly on Ben's office door, poked her head around it in imitation of his brief appearance at her door earlier, and said briefly, 'The Dredges have arrived. Would you like to go and say all the right things while I ring and warn sister?'

Before he could answer, she quickly withdrew, and was in her office waiting for someone to answer the phone at the wards when he hurried past towards the front entrance.

She took her time speaking to the nurse who at last answered the phone, and then slowly picked up the set of new charts, and strolled back to the foyer.

'Ah, there you are, Miss Provis.'

Ben turned towards her with a glint in his eye that told her he knew exactly why she had suggested he meet the new arrivals.

'Miss Burgess is going to join me in the visitors' lounge-room for a cup of coffee while you talk privately to Mr and Mrs Dredge,' he turned the tables on her smoothly, his eyes daring her to suggest otherwise.

Miss Burgess was looking at the handsome man as though she would like to eat him alive. Then she turned her eyes to find Ellena watching her. A slight flush rose in her cheeks, but she looked down her nose as though nurses, even directors of nursing, were well beneath her social standing.

Ellena smiled brightly. 'Excellent! I'll no doubt meet you again, Miss Burgess.'

She nodded her dismissal, avoiding Ben's face, and sat down near the couple, deliberately ignoring the two still standing.

She was very conscious of Ben's feelings as she heard

his controlled voice say, 'If you would follow me, Miss Burgess?'

'Oh, do call me Annabel,' Ellena heard the woman gush as they moved away.

A cheerful-faced EN arrived a little later with a wheelchair, just after Ellena had almost finished asking about Mr Dredge's nursing history. She noted that Mr Dredge glared from the nurse to the wheelchair.

Ellena introduced them, and was delighted when the nurse proffered her hand politely to each one. She knew how much this old-fashioned courtesy often meant to elderly people.

'Won't be a moment, Jill,' she beamed approvingly at the nurse, and quickly finished her queries about their new patient's sleeping habits at home.

'Right, that will do for now,' she said briskly at last, 'Sister will finish this later before you leave, Mrs Dredge. And now, sir, what about a ride in the wheelchair just for this morning? I'm sure you'd like to see over the complex with your wife, and there's quite a lot of it to see. Then I'm afraid it will be back to your own two feet.'

She noticed his expression lighten and he willingly let his wife and Ellena help him to his feet. Then once again he couldn't move.

'Ever been taught to rock when that happens, Mr Dredge?' Ellena said lightly.

The puzzled look on his wife's face was answer enough before his slow, 'No. . .no. . .like my feet are glued to the carpet,' he said in a soft monotone.

'OK, your very first lesson. Would you mind if Jill helps me for a moment, Mrs Dredge?'

When Jill had quickly exchanged places, they both held him firmly as Ellena explained.

'We're just going to rock you gently back and forth on your feet and it should help. Ready?'

They gently rocked the rigid figure forward and back a few times.

'Now lift your left foot. Right foot. Ah. . .'

After a couple of attempts he had suddenly moved easily forward several feet.

'Fine. That will do this time. Jill, if you would slide the chair behind Mr Dredge, please.'

Ellena waved to them both cheerfully as they moved off, happy and relieved to see that now a hint of excitement and anticipation had replaced most of the apprehension in the old dears' faces.

But ten minutes later, Ellena was staring at a serious ambulance officer with increasing dismay, and then mounting fury, as he told her about the second admission he had just brought to the complex.

CHAPTER SEVEN

'I. . .I THOUGHT I should mention it, Miss Provis,' Dan said anxiously. 'I remember once before you said something about not allowing patients like this one into your new set-up here. I even mentioned it to the sister at the isolation ward when I was so surprised the patient for Macallister's was in there. But she assured me that, when she rang to let you know how the patient was progressing that Dr Gill had seen and agreed to take at a later date, the DON here said you would take him immediately, had seen no problem about it. I knew you'd been away and I tried to get her to ring you again but she was frantically busy and. . .er. . . got quite stroppy!'

What am I going to do? Ellena thought frantically. The patient had already been travelling for well over an hour from out west, and was no doubt already very weary. Too weary to make the return trip. If his bed had not already been filled! A shortage of beds was no doubt why they had wanted him in rehab for fitting of his prosthesis even before the suture line had healed.

She looked again at the nursing transfer letter. There it was. Written in black and white.

'As previously notified. . .'

And then a concise report followed. Not of a neurological disorder, but of an unstabilised diabetic with peripheral arterial damage so that his leg had been amputated below the knee. The wound had become infected with the multi-resistant-to-antibiotic strain of the staphylococcus bacteria. One of the curses of modern hospitals!

'Do you think Mr Campbell could stay in the ambulance while I try and work something out, Dan?'

'No problem. Do you think I could take out a bite to eat for him?'

Ellena quickly rang the kitchen and an obliging voice willingly agreed to provide morning tea and take it out for the officer and his diabetic patient.

As soon as Dan had gone back to his ambulance parked right up to the front door, Ellena tried to contact Dr James Gill. He was not at the hospital, she was informed by the woman on the switchboard, but she agreed to page him for her on his long-range beeper.

As she hung up, Ellena hoped fervently that he was already on his way to admit both patients. As long as he knew about them! There just had not been time in the busy morning to fit in a phone call to check. Then she pushed away her desire to handle this by herself, knowing she would at least need a witness, and headed for the small lounge-room at the other end of the wards.

She firmly stifled the pang that rose when she heard Ben's infectious laugh as she approached. Her wayward heart sank when she saw that he had been genuinely kept amused by his beautiful companion.

'I'm sorry to interrupt, Mr Nicoletti,' she blurted out rapidly, 'but we have a problem.'

The smile on his face disappeared and he stood up quickly when he saw her face, despite the loud protest from Annabel.

'Something you can't handle again, Miss Provis,' he said quite nastily.

She felt too upset to rise to his baiting, and noted his intent look when she only nodded briefly, and muttered, 'The other new admission,' before turning to his haughty companion. 'If you would excuse us, Miss Burgess? You should find your in-laws in room twelve still. Or,' she hastened to add as the beautiful features hardened, 'you could stay here, if you wish to wait.'

'Oh, Bennie has already so kindly offered to look after Mother for me.' She beamed up at Ben as she rose quickly. 'And I really must get back to the television studio,' she added importantly.

She insisted on accompanying them, tottering slowly along on her high heels with her arm tucked in Ben's elbow, while Ellena was forced to walk slowly behind and to listen to them finalising arrangements to meet the next evening at one of the newest restaurants in Newcastle. She refused to admit her annoyance with them both for so completely ignoring her was based in sheer jealousy, dismissing the thought angrily.

Ben did, however, manage to dexterously get rid of the woman still clinging to him when he saw the ambulance.

'Well?' he snapped as he followed Ellena at last into her office.

'MRSA.'

He looked startled as she angrily thrust the new patient's papers into his hands.

'I don't understand too much medical jargon,' he snapped again. 'Explain.'

'But you've heard of golden staph?'

When he nodded, she continued rapidly, 'Another name is methicillin-resistant staphlococcus aureus or MRSA. A recent national survey of seven and a half thousand golden staph strains isolated from Australian hospitals found that over eighty-five per cent were resistant to penicillin. It's now nearly useless against this major source of infection in hospitals. Hospital-acquired infections such as MRSA have been estimated to kill up to five hundred Australians a year and make many others seriously ill.'

'Get to the point.'

'The point is that Dr Hansen laid down very strict guidelines about admission of patients directly from large hospitals to his rehabilitation complex! MRSA is something hospital administrators hate to think about, let alone talk about! But he insisted from the start that every patient with an infected lesion had to be cleared by pathology tests of any MRSA before being accepted for admission. We still even have to take pathology swabs of nose, groin and throat of any admission straight from large hospitals. Even new staff have to be cleared as not being carriers. He wants us to do our utmost to keep it out of here as long as possible!'

Comprehension was beginning to dawn on Ben's face.

'Sister Linda Terry again?' he said through gritted teeth.

'We have a large wound full of MRSA on a diabetic patient who has already been in that ambulance over an hour! And the acting DON was warned, but was reported as seeing no problem in admitting him today!'

This time her worry was so deep, it barely registered when he smoothed down the moustache a couple of times with agitated fingers as she watched him anxiously.

'So we can't admit him,' he said flatly at last as he raised his eyes from the papers in his hands.

'I've paged Dr Gill on his long-range beeper, but

do you know if there's any way we can contact Chris?'

He shook his head regretfully. 'Chris will be in London still. As soon as his father-in-law's condition was found not to be as bad as first thought, he flew over late to an important medical conference. He didn't want to go without Jean and while George was recuperating, but Jean put her foot down. I'd rather not worry her with this. Do you have any suggestions?'

'Oh, dear! I'd forgotten all about that trip overseas!' She noticed his eyes narrow slightly as she paused. 'I had thought he might speak to the referring consultant and explain,' she said with a sigh. 'Well, James will just have to contact the hospital resident doctor where the patient has just come from, and he may be able to contact the consultant, who just may agree to him being admitted to a local hospital until he's free of MRSA. If there's a spare bed anywhere and they will agree to take him,' Ellena added slowly.

'Couldn't you ring the doctor yourself and explain the situation?'

She grimaced. 'Some consultants don't like mere nurses ringing them about something like this. Especially this doctor, from the little I've had to do with him.'

'Well, if he won't agree we'll have to think of something,' Ben said grimly. 'I'll go and have a word with the ambulance driver.'

Before she could explain the driver's part in letting her know before the patient had been carried in, Ben had disappeared.

He returned a few minutes later. 'No word from James?' he asked, grim-faced.

She shook her head. 'I'm just hoping he's already on his way here.'

'Well, he'd better be,' he said briefly. 'The ambu-

lance base was just on to our driver asking why he
was still here. He said he won't be able to stall them
much longer without getting into trouble himself.'

'There's still something I don't understand.'

'I think I can guess what it is,' he sighed as he sat
down and ran a hand agitatedly through his hair. 'Why
did Linda tell me this guy had neurological problems?'

She nodded anxiously. 'I'm just hoping we don't
have another patient about to arrive as well, unless
the note was mixed up with information about Mr
Dredge.'

'Could be, but I doubt it. Our Sister Terry told me
about him when she handed me that note. Besides,
the name is right, and so is the referring doctor's name.
It will be interesting to hear what she has to say about
this when she comes back from days off,' he added
grimly.

Linda Terry had quite a lot to say when challenged
about the new admission on her return from days off.

'Of course I wasn't told about the MRSA!' she
declared furiously. 'That's a load of garbage! I wrote
down what was told me. Neurological disorder!'

Ellena looked at her steadily, wondering whether to
believe her or not. 'Did you know Macallister's MRSA
policy for new admissions?'

There was the faintest hesitation before she looked
Ellena straight in the eye and snapped, 'I told you I
had read the protocol.'

'Yes, so you did, Sister,' Ellena said very slowly,
remembering also very clearly how she had misrepresented her to Ben.

No, she realised now, not just misrepresented. Linda
Terry had lied then. And suddenly Ellena knew she

was lying now. She had known about the MRSA. And perhaps she had chosen to ignore the protocol again.

Something was going on here, and Ellena stared at the defiant woman for a long moment before at last saying strongly, 'Well, make sure you document all information about new admissions even more carefully in the future. And not on a scrap of paper such as you gave Mr Nicoletti. Use the admission book. Fortunately there was a local bed available for that patient. He will only be coming to us when his wound is healed and he's clear of MRSA. But the whole episode was most embarrassing for us. It didn't help us establish credibility for this new venture.'

Ellena stood up and walked forward and opened the door.

'By the way, I know I said I'd try and show you some basic rehab techniques. Unfortunately, I still have far too much work to catch up on. I've asked Nurse Pleasant to show you correct chair transfers and walking with a pylon this shift and. . .is something the matter, Sister?'

Linda was scowling. 'It's just to get your own back, isn't it?' she snarled.

'I beg your pardon?'

Suddenly Ellena wished she had agreed to allowing Ben to be present at this interview. He had stated he believed he should be present, but had fallen short of insisting, perhaps reluctant to damage the friendlier relationship that had been developing between them.

'You're just trying to humiliate me in front of the other staff! Telling an EN to teach me! Me! Why, I've been the DON. Doing *your* work. And now you're telling everyone I don't know what I'm doing! I kept this place going. *And* while you were off having a ball!'

There was a feverish flush under the heavy make-up. But it was the glittering, flashing eyes that rang warning bells for Ellena. She winced inwardly, but outwardly was well in control.

'Sister Terry, that's enough!' Ben's unexpected voice from the doorway cracked like a whip. 'If you're not happy with the work here and what's now expected of you, you are quite at liberty to resign.'

'Thank you, Mr Nicoletti, but I'm the one who appoints my staff,' Ellena said coldly, and deliberately turned her back on him. 'Sister Terry, I will not have RNs in charge of shifts who are not able to supervise the rest of the staff in even such a basic area as correct chair transfers! Alison Pleasant worked for many years in geriatric rehabilitation in Sydney. We were very fortunate to be able to employ her as she is one of the most experienced practical rehab nurses we have. There is no other RN rostered on with you tonight. I've been working twelve-hour days, and have several things to finish this evening again before I can leave as it is. Now, if you will excuse me. . .?'

'You'd like me to resign, wouldn't you? But you're not going to get rid of me after all the hard work I've put in. I'll get you for this! See if I don't!'

The words were hissed softly, but so venomously, that Ellena took a step back, and then the contorted face changed dramatically as Linda moved past her towards Ben, still standing some distance away.

'I'm sorry, Ben. I've really done everything I could, but apparently it still wasn't good enough.' Tears filled Linda's eyes.

Ben strode forward, and smiled at Linda. 'I know you have,' he murmured soothingly, to Ellena's disgust.

'Th-thanks Ben.' A tremulous smile chased away the tears. 'And I'm looking forward very much to tomorrow night. How on earth did you get tickets to the Civic Theatre in Newcastle at such short notice?'

Both thumbs on Ben's well shaped hands pointed triumphantly upwards.

'It's not what you know. . .'

'. . .but who you know!'

The two finished in a chorus as they beamed at each other before Ellena's disbelieving eyes.

'Just think, Ellena, this dear, dear man remembered I'm a fan of Victor Borge and rang me last night to say he had two tickets. I adore Borge's shows. They're a real scream.'

'It's a shame you're working a quick shift, though,' Ben said, not taking his eyes off the animated face. 'I hope you won't be *too* tired tomorrow night.'

Linda actually gurgled with laughter.

'Never!' she pronounced gaily. She turned and smiled at Ellena. 'I'm sure I'll be able to get off on time for such an important date, won't I, Ellena?' Her eyes were now hard and challenging. The only hint of amusement in them malicious and triumphant.

Ellena took a deep breath, her hands clenched into fists, but before she could say a word, Ben said confidently, 'Oh, I'm sure you will, Linda, love. But we'd both better get on with it now.'

His smile disappeared completely as he looked for the first time at the DON. 'Do you have a moment, Miss Provis? I've a problem with several of the timesheets. And if we can't sort it out I'll find it difficult to get away on time myself, or there'll be staff telling me I've paid them the wrong amounts in their pay.'

'Oh, dear! Poor you!' Linda gushed sympathetically

at Ellena. 'It *is* difficult getting it all right after such a long time away on holidays, isn't it? Never mind, I'm sure you'll be all sorted out by next week. Must go.' Another sparkling smile was flashed at Ben before she turned and strode purposefully away.

Ellena felt frozen in disbelief. Ben had shared her anger and suspicion of Linda Terry. Yet he had gone out of his way to make a date with her?

Hurt ripped through her. She turned abruptly away in case he saw the tears that had sprung to her eyes. Then she was angry with herself. Hadn't she already known well enough that dark-featured, handsome men were faithless and worthless? And yet she had been letting those barriers against being hurt start to slide.

'I really would appreciate it if you could check these timetables more thoroughly than this before they come to my office,' Ben said accusingly as he followed her into her office.

Ellena forced herself to concentrate on the sheets he spread out on her desk, refusing to remind him that all the shifts of the previous fortnight should have been signed by Sister Terry.

'I'm sorry, Mr Nicoletti,' she managed to say steadily.

She pulled out the previous roster to make sure that the staff had filled out the right times.

'Do you have to check them that thoroughly?' he snapped impatiently. 'Couldn't you just sign them?'

'No,' she said in a stifled voice, grasping desperately for control.

And she had actually started to like this man! Started to wonder if after all he might be different from. . . from. . .

There was a stillness about him as she seated herself

and bent over the desk, hiding her face from him as
she began to check without another word. Then he
moved impatiently towards the door.

'Well, give them to my secretary again when you've
finished,' he snapped angrily.

She looked up and watched his stiff back disappear
with bewilderment. What on earth had changed him
so suddenly from the man she had grown to admire
immensely during the last couple of days?

Even a few hours ago at lunchtime he had asked
her if she minded his going outside with her for a
breath of fresh air. Together they had wandered for a
brief time along the edge of the lake in perfect accord,
not feeling the need to say much, just allowing the
brisk breeze to blow into their faces, releasing the
tension that had built up in them from the frantic pace
of the morning.

He had sighed as they had at last re-approached the
cream brick building and the various problems they
each had to deal with.

She had turned and smiled gently at him as she said,
'That was a big sigh. It would be nice to spend more
time out here, wouldn't it?'

He had nodded briefly, his eyes looking across
the lake.

'It would be nice to be able to do a lot of things,'
he'd muttered almost to himself.

Then he had suddenly stood still and grasped her
elbow. She had thought his voice sounded strained and
urgent as he'd started to speak.

'Ellena, there's——'

'Hi, Mr Nicoletti, Miss Provis.'

Bob, the groundsman, general handyman and determined gardener, had appeared around the bank of

azaleas. By the time they had greeted him and willingly admired the dark pink camellia shrub he had just planted, the moment was lost, and they had hurried back to their respective tasks.

Well, she decided now as she forced herself to continue checking the papers in front of her, if he could change that fast, dear Linda—'Linda, love'—was welcome to him!

And that belief was strengthened during the days that followed.

It seemed some days that there was nothing that Ellena could do to satisfy the administrator. He was in her office snarling at her about the most trivial things, and usually when one of the staff was within earshot. She only occasionally caught a glimpse of the warm, caring person she had begun to think he was. And, during that time, Linda became more and more assertive and unpopular with staff and patients on the wards.

In all fairness to the woman, there were some days when she seemed to be a good nurse. But she was very erratic, and on bad days was sharp, caustic and irritable, and almost feverish in pushing herself and the nurses on duty with her, until the atmosphere could have been cut with a knife.

Unfortunately no one made an official complaint, and Linda must have been particularly careful around the DON so that she didn't again catch her in any serious breach. So Ellena's hands were tied. Even if she had received an official complaint, it no doubt would have still ended up being Sister Terry's word against her accuser's. Ellena felt increasingly frustrated and helpless. Strangely enough, there had not even been any more complaints from the patients, although Linda obviously remained very unpopular.

And as Ellena's relationship with Ben continued to deteriorate, it really bewildered her that he was all smiles with Linda Terry.

Ellena did her best to ignore what was happening, but some deep part of her felt torn and bruised. No matter how she upbraided herself, she could not forget those far too brief moments when there had been such closeness of mind and purpose between herself and Ben.

Although Linda had never come right out and said Ben was dating her, she made so many snide comments within Ellena's hearing that she had to face the fact that they were going out together. To Ellena's disgust, this knowledge caused her many nights spent tossing and turning in her lonely bed. And there were far too many times when she looked at Ben and wondered if Linda was enjoying his kisses. She tried her utmost to ignore them both, but she never quite managed to repair adequately the dent in her armour, and there were many barbs from Linda that hit their mark.

But the days flew by as she dealt with each difficulty as it arose with her usual calm efficiency. Never once did she again let anyone see her upset or unduly ruffled. Tears and anger were kept for those solitary times in her flat. Or, when the walls seemed to press in on her with the memories of Gran and Howard, she took long walks in the cool evenings, returning to collapse into bed and sleep from sheer exhaustion.

Despite the tension that usually seemed to build up on the shifts Linda worked, the staff was much happier as the place returned to normal. Several patients were making excellent progress in becoming more independent, especially with Mrs Davis after a week on the anti-depressant medication, less sleep in daylight hours and less night sedation, and persistent reinforcement of ADL drills.

James Gill had done several very long rounds, including one that first day after sorting out the new admissions, leaving Ellena still rather puzzled why he had done such brief, unsatisfactory ones the two weeks previously. He was a very thorough, conscientious young doctor, if a little pedantic. Most of their elderly patients had multiple health problems, and he painstakingly went through their medical history notes one by one.

This resulted in a multitude of tests ordered, from full blood counts, blood bio-chemistries to X-rays. A couple of patients had been complaining of pain. A gastroscopy was ordered for a man with a suspected ulcer from anti-inflammatory medications. And Ellena had managed to convince James to order a follow-up X-ray on a supposedly healed fractured neck of femur that had been to Theatre several weeks before for a pin and plate.

The old lady had continuously complained of severe pain in her hip preventing her from full weight bearing on that leg. Some of the staff, especially Linda, had reported that they believed she was only malingering and not trying hard enough to mobilise on her walking frame. Even injections of pethidine had not relieved some bouts, although that had rather puzzled the staff. Why would the injections be effective some times more than others?

Ellena was in the middle of doing her round of the patients when James rang her with Mrs Richards' X-ray result.

'Your suspicions were right, Ellena,' he said briskly,

'one of the screws on the plate has migrated out of position, no doubt causing soft tissue damage. I'll ring her orthopaedic doctor who did the original op, and arrange an appointment for her.'

Linda was hovering near the desk when Ellena thoughtfully hung up. It was one of several annoying habits of the RN, obviously trying to listen in to phone conversations.

'Oh, Sister Terry, as you must have heard,' Ellena could not prevent her slightly ascerbic tone, 'Mrs Richards' X-ray has shown a problem. She is not to weight-bear at all until we have instructions from her orthopaedic specialist.'

She pulled out the patient's chart, and was about to note the phoned instructions when she realised Linda had not moved.

She glanced up at her, and then tensed at the furious expression on her face.

'So! Miss Perfect's right again! You. . .you. . .'

The woman seemed to become speechless with rage.

'Sister Terry!'

Before Ellena could get more than that outraged exclamation out, Joan Wheat appeared around the corner at the end of the corridor.

Linda spotted her at the same time. 'Of course, Miss Provis, I'll attend to Mrs Richards right away,' the RN said a shade too loudly, and then turned and strode hurriedly away in the other direction.

Ellena hesitated, staring with astonishment at her disappearing figure. Not for the first time did Ellena wonder if something was wrong with the woman. There were times she even seemed irrational.

'Anything wrong, Ellena?' Joan said with a frown, as she reached the desk, her eyes following Linda.

Should she tell the other RN her suspicions? Perhaps others had noted something? Ellena hesitated, and then gave a strained smile. As before, no one else had heard, and once again it was her word against the other woman's.

'Just a bit of her usual unpleasantness, I'm afraid,' she said slowly. 'Let's see if we can finish this round before we get any more interruptions, shall we?' she added briskly.

But it was not to be.

Ellena had been so thankful that morning that it was Friday, and the next morning she could sleep in. She was very weary. There was still far too much work for one person, but Ben had at last been persuaded the previous week to advertise for a deputy director.

Ellena had not been able to understand his reluctance to do so, and in the end had been forced to insist. That had been another occasion for him to be very sarcastic and hurtful about her ability to cope. And, once again, Linda had been within earshot. As far as Ellena knew there had been a couple of enquiries, but the position had to be advertised at least one more time.

This morning as she had commenced her round of the patients, she had dreaded the thought that Linda was again working both Saturday and Sunday when she herself was off duty.

And now, after Linda's almost irrational behaviour this morning, she was wondering even more worriedly whether she should go into the office again on Saturday morning to catch up on some paperwork and keep an eye on Linda for a couple of hours.

Then Alison Pleasant called her again to the phone.

This time it was Ellena's solicitor.

CHAPTER EIGHT

'THE land and stock agent thinks he may have a buyer for the farm, Miss Provis.'

The solicitor's voice was very cheerful, seemingly insensitive to the heartache his words would cause.

Ellena sank down slowly on to the chair at the nurses' station. She was vaguely aware that Alison Pleasant glanced up at her sharply, and paused for a moment before bending again to continue writing on a chart.

'Do. . .do you know who it is?' she forced herself to ask softly.

Ellena sat frozen, the phone clenched in her hand until the knuckles were white. So it had come at last.

'A wealthy businessman from Sydney is looking for a farm in the area, and seems very taken with your well grassed property with the tree-lined creek supplying plenty of water,' the man's voice echoed in her ears. 'But he's made an offer of several thousand less than the agent had been hoping to get.'

A Sydney businessman. A hobby farmer?

Her grandmother had often been scathing about city slickers with too much money who thought it might be fun to own a farm. Pitt Street farmers, she had called them. Too many times they neglected the land and animals dreadfully once the novelty wore off or the money ran out.

'I'd like to meet him before I give an answer,' she said shakily at last.

The solicitor hesitated. 'I'm not sure if that will be possible. Apparently he was here last weekend, and I'm not sure when he'll be up again.'

'Please have the estate agent tell him I refuse to make a decision until I meet him,' she said decisively. 'If he can't meet me all the way out at the farm this weekend, perhaps he could make a trip to Lake Macquarie some time. Even if it has to be during working hours.'

Suddenly it seemed very important that the person who bought the property would really care about the land and the house. That would be the last thing she would be able to do for the generations who had loved the place.

She sat for a moment after the call was disconnected, her eyes closed, filled again with the devastating anguish she had not allowed creep up on her since the evening she had met Ben.

There had been only Ellena to make all the final arrangements for her grandmother's funeral. And all through the sad service, deep down had been that desolate feeling of knowing she was now totally alone in the world with no one any longer to belong to. That feeling had increased and mingled with fear and anxiety during the weeks and horrible days of sorting and clearing out the equipment on the property ready for an auction, as well as the old homestead that had been her only real home.

Her grandmother had talked it all over with her quite calmly and rationally during that last week. Almost as though she had known, Ellena had realised later. Gran had apparently long ago accepted the fact that one day the farm would have to be sold. And even if Ellena had wanted to keep it, it wouldn't have been feasible to have someone else manage it.

With her being the sole beneficiary of her grandmother's will, the solicitors had gone through all the business relating to the farm very thoroughly, filling in several gaps Gran had not explained fully.

Oh, Ellena had known times were tough, but it had been a tremendous shock to find out how much Gran had kept from her over the years. There had even been considerable money still owing on a loan that she had known nothing about. Once Gran had been forced to have to restock after a disastrous drought ten years before. In fact, it had been the year after that farce of a marriage ceremony with Howard—after the court case. Gran had never given her a hint that she was low on funds when she had insisted on paying for that top barrister to protect her granddaughter from the charge of accessory to Howard's prohibited drug dealing.

But it all boiled down to the fact that there was simply no money available, and nothing Ellena could do to make it possible to hang on to the property that had been bought originally by Ellena's great grandfather. The state of the rural economy had drained all resources dry and she was assured there was no alternative than to sell up.

The first sale she had organised had been of all the stock. The dairy herd built up over good years had shrunk considerably, but it had still been a tremendous wrench to watch what remained trucked away to the sale yards. Only her faithful old horse, Whippy, had not been sold, and only because she had managed to get a neighbour to agree to look after him at a price. The only good thing about the sale was that there might be sufficient money left to buy a couple of acres on the outskirts of Newcastle. Somewhere where she would be able to have. . .

'Are you OK, Miss Provis?' a soft voice asked hesitantly.

Ellena straightened, not looking at the EN.

'Yes, thank you, Alison.'

She rose stiffly and walked blindly away to the staff-room, unaware of the still anxious, puzzled expression on the face of the kind-hearted young woman.

Ellena was vaguely thankful that the staff-room was empty as she quickly made her way through it to the small rest-room cubicle. Suddenly it was all too much. Gran. Ben. And she was just so weary. Then the sobs rose up and ripped through her.

'Miss Provis?'

Ellena wasn't sure how long she had been crying before she heard the soft, hesitant voice and vainly tried to stifle the next sob.

'Is there anything I can do?' the RN persisted.

Ellena fought for control as she recognised Joan Wheat's voice. It was a couple of moments before she was able to call back in a low voice still husky from the bout of tears.

'No. I. . .I. . .it's just a personal matter, Joan, thank you. I'll be back to finish my round later.'

There was silence for a moment, and then she heard the door swish closed. She took a few deep quivering breaths and at last made her way unsteadily to the hand basin. After splashing cold water on her face a few times, she at last reluctantly dared to look in the mirror, knowing what she would see.

'Oh, why do I always look such a wreck after crying?' she muttered frantically as she stared with horror at the puffed-up eyelids and red-streaked eyes.

'All I need is for Sister Terry to see the DON like this!'

There was no way she could let *anyone* see her like this!

She splashed more water on her face, dried it carefully, and then shrugged helplessly at her appearance. Well, there was no help for it. She couldn't stay there any longer.

There was no one in the corridor. No one looked up at her as she strode swiftly past the lounge, and she breathed a sigh of relief as she turned the last corner.

But her luck didn't last. Ben met her just as she reached the office door. But then she quickly realised it wasn't her bad luck but Joan's interference.

'Ellena, whatever's the matter? Sister Wheat said you were crying.'

His voice was nothing like the hard, sharp one she had only seemed to have heard lately. It was filled with anxiety. It was seductive, gentle, and sent shivers through her defenceless body.

She groaned inwardly, keeping her face averted as she strode past him.

'I've a couple of things to do, Mr Nicoletti. . .' like putting on camouflage make-up and not allowing your kindness to affect me like this '. . .and I'll be right with. . .with. . .'

She gulped as his hand shot out and grabbed her by the elbow. He twisted her towards him, and then at last she looked defiantly up at him.

'Oh, Ellena. . .Ellie. . .'

She thought for a fraught moment that it must be her imagination that there was sudden anguish in his voice as he saw her tear-ravaged face. Then he was

pushing her gently further into the room and closing
and locking the door.

Then, wonder of wonders, gentle hands were pulling
her close, his hoarse voice beginning to soothe her as
the tears started trickling down her cheeks again.

Without conscious thought she rested her head
against his broad shoulder and his arms tightened
around her. And she had been right. He was just the
right height for her. She felt his head press against
hers, then his lips on her temple.

He seemed so familiar. Like coming home. He had
even called her Ellie. Gran had been the only one who
had ever called her that. Without any thought her arms
reached for him and clung.

And quite suddenly she knew.

Knew why the thought of him with Linda or anyone
else had disturbed her so much. Knew it wasn't just
the thought of her authority being undermined. Knew
how stupid she had been not to realise weeks ago that
the pain his treatment of her had brought was not
because of professional hurt, but heart-hurt.

Quite simply, she loved him with all her being.

'Has that woman been upsetting you more than
usual?' he said at last in a fierce voice.

For a moment she was still so caught up in the
sudden knowledge and wonder of loving this man that
what he had said hardly registered.

Then she stiffened, and started to pull away.

'No, stay there,' he protested, his arms tightening.

For a moment she yielded to the sheer delight of
his nearness a moment longer, then she raised her head
reluctantly.

'If by "that woman" you mean Linda Terry she's
never stopped upsetting me,' her husky voice said

bitterly as she stared into his dark eyes.

His arms slowly loosened. She pulled away again, and he let her go.

But not far. A clean handkerchief was in his hand and he reached out and started mopping up her face. Mesmerised, she felt him. . .oh, so gently. . .trace the tears down her cheeks, her eyes lost in studying his worried expression. A series of expressions flashed across his face that she couldn't quite make out. Frustration? Guilt? Anger?

'Why don't you sack her, then?'

Her eyes narrowed. 'And deprive you of your girlfriend?'

Sudden surprise filled his face. 'Girlfriend!' he said in a stunned voice, and then his eyes darkened with fury.

Her chin went up and she held his gaze. 'I can't fire anyone unless they have received at least two warnings for misdemeanours,' she said abruptly. 'The main cause for instant dismissal is proof of patient abuse. And she has stopped short of that, thank goodness,' she added bitterly.

Some of the anger went out of his face. He opened his mouth, and then obviously changed his mind.

'Why were you crying?' he said very quietly.

'Well, it certainly wasn't because of Sister Terry!'

Even as Ellena moved shakily away from him, she knew that wasn't entirely true. It hadn't just been the phone call, and the stirring up of those painful memories. It had simply been everything. Ben. Linda. The workload. That lonely flat at the end of each day. And the fact that she loved someone who didn't return that love.

The African violets had not faltered in their new

home. It was only a few weeks since she had put them there, but it felt like months. Ellena stared at them sadly. Hardly realising what she was doing, she reached out and picked up the old china plant pot. The one she had herself given Gran when she had received her very first pay packet. She clutched it tightly as she raised her eyes and stared blindly out on to the nearby car park.

Oh, Gran, if only I could talk to you! Tell you this man has such a weird effect on me. I've fallen in love with him. And yet. . .how can I have? At first he seemed only another handsome, self-opinionated man like Howard. He's even been so horrible to work with most of the time.

There had been several clashes with Ben. He had bowled ahead and given orders. He'd purchased equipment without consulting her until she was close to erupting. It was obvious that he was used to being in sole charge and seemed to conveniently forget her own responsibilities. She'd found out that for the last few years he had been planning to get into health administration, but his business had not been ready to leave when this complex had commenced.

But despite all that. . .despite his arrogance at times, there was something about him. Something strong. Something solid but tempered with compassion, to everyone but Ellena, it had seemed sometimes. The patients and staff, almost without exception, thought the world of him. It had often seemed to her that she was the only one he didn't like, that she aggravated him for some unknown reason. How that knowledge stung!

But even then, once or twice after he had been particularly harsh to her she had thought she had

caught a glimpse of something like regret in his
eyes. . .pain. . .

But, oh, how she had treasured—even while it bewildered her—those infinitely precious few times when
they had worked very harmoniously together. Times
when she had recognised a similar thought pattern to
her own. Times when he had been so. . .so nice to her.

Like when she had rearranged the staff rosters. He'd
never said a word to her about the damage it had done
to their budget. Thank goodness she had managed to
convince a few of the staff, who had originally been
persuaded by Linda to take their annual leaves the
fortnight after her return, to postpone them. And a
few had returned from leave, so that since then there
had only been need for only a few extra casual hours.

Once she'd even thought she had noticed a tender
light in his eyes when she had turned away from trying
to cajole Mrs Davis into making an effort to walk a
little further on her pylon one day. But he had quickly
swung round, and she had known she must have been
mistaken when he snapped at her harshly a moment
later. It had been in front of Linda too, who had openly
gloated once again.

The sharp ring of the phone startled her out of
her daze.

Before she could move she heard Ben answer it with
a terse, 'Yes?'

Then she swung around as she heard him say with
ice in his voice, 'No, Sister Terry, Miss Provis is not
available! I'm sure you are perfectly capable of managing that by yourself. In fact, Miss Provis is leaving for
home very shortly.'

She made a startled denial, and his face lifted
towards her. For a moment the ferocity of his whole

face frightened her. Then she realised it wasn't directed at her, but at the person on the other end of the phone as he snarled into it!

'No! You may not come to her office. Are you deaf, woman?' he roared suddenly, and flung the phone down.

Then he had reached Ellena's side in a couple of strides. He took the pot-plant from her and plonked it back on the windowsill. Then his hand grasped her wrist.

'Quick! Where's your bag?'

Before she could move, he spotted it on top of a cupboard. Pulling her after him, he moved like lightning to grab it, then began hauling her towards the door.

'Where. . .? I can't——'

'If we aren't out of here in two seconds flat that menace'll find some reason to come here. Just to gloat again over your distress! And I've reached the end of it!'

Menace! Was that any way to speak of. . .? And then she was almost running to keep up as he dragged her along with him. Then they were out of the front door.

But the way still wasn't clear.

'Oh, Bennie, darling,' Ellena heard, with horror, Miss Burgess's pleased tones say, 'you're just the man I——'

'Sorry, Miss Burgess. Emergency!' Ben snapped without pausing.

Then Ellena was rushed past, and they were almost running across the car park. She was breathless and in shock as he bundled her into his car.

'You. . .we. . .I can't just leave like this!' she managed to squeak in outraged tones.

'Can't you? Just watch!' he snarled.

The car roared past Miss Burgess still standing just outside the main entrance. A second woman jolted to a stop beside her as Ellena looked back.

For a fleeting moment she saw the same look of fury on both faces as Linda Terry and the TV celebrity watched them.

Then the car had swung on to the main road and they were lost to sight.

'I don't think I believe this!'

Still in a daze, she stared across at Ben. His hands were gripped on the wheel, his lips a thin line. He glanced briefly at her, and his expression softened a little.

'You will.'

'Where. . .why. . .?'

She swallowed, trying to regain control of her voice.

'Somewhere we can talk without interruption.'

'We could have done that in my office!'

'Not with Linda Terry pounding on the door any moment!'

She subsided, desperately wondering what he wanted to talk about. She still hadn't told him what had upset her. Goodness knew what he was thinking was the cause!

What could she say? she thought a little hysterically. 'I was crying because life was just too hard all round for a little while'? or perhaps, 'I was crying because there's no one who loves me any more'?

Ellena shuddered.

A large hand reached across and tucked one of hers into it. She looked down at their linked hands and then she felt the warmth. The comfort. Her fingers tightened until she was clinging to him.

Neither said a word for a long time. Ellena found herself gradually relaxing, still clinging to his hand. Hope and excitement were rising. Surely he would never call a woman he. . .he loved a 'menace'!

Then the car slowed, and they were bouncing up a short driveway and pulling to a stop.

Ben turned to her and smiled.

The beauty and tenderness of it made her catch her breath in sheer wonder. His other hand reached across and a fingertip gently touched her cheek. But as he opened his mouth, a door slammed near by, and dismay filled his face as he groaned.

'Oh, no. I thought——'

'Why, Benedetto! What on earth are you doing home so early?'

The voice was slightly accented. Italian, Ellena suspected, and she frantically tugged her hands free as a face appeared at the window.

The hair was liberally sprinkled with grey, but it had the same luxurious, curling thickness of Ben's. The same thick black eyebrows shot up as dark eyes examined Ellena.

'Ah ha! This must be the young lady who has been causing so much trouble!'

Ben said something sharply in a foreign language.

As he opened his door and started around to Ellena's side the woman answered him with a stream of words. Then he was helping Ellena out of the car, and she turned nervously to face the short, stout woman who had fallen silent. Her hands now rested on her hips as she watched Ellena through narrowed eyes.

'This is Chris and Jean's director of nursing, Ellena Irene Provis,' Ben said shortly. 'Ellena, this is my mother.'

'As I said, the woman who has been causing you so much trouble,' Mrs Nicoletti said with confidence, and then her whole face lit up with a mischievous smile so reminiscent of Ben's that Ellena could only stare.

'How—how do you do, Mrs Nicoletti?' Ellena stammered.

'I am much, much better for having met you at last,' the attractive, deep voice said softly.

She grinned at her exasperated son—no, more like embarrassed son, Ellena realised—and then turned to lead the way into the house.

'Well, all mothers do like to meet the woman in their son's life,' she tossed over her shoulder.

Ellena stopped dead. 'I. . .I'm afraid you're mistaken. I'm not——'

'Don't be shy, darling,' Ben's voice said in her ear.

Pain ripped through her. Longing to be truly his darling seared her. Before she could think of another word, she felt her elbow gripped and once again he was propelling her forward.

Mrs Nicoletti led them into a bright, comfortably furnished lounge. Ben threw more words at his mother that Ellena couldn't understand, and she miserably tugged her arm free and moved away.

'That's enough, Ben,' his mother interrupted firmly. 'We are being very rude to your guest. I was just on my way over to your brother's house, so I'll leave you to look after Ellena.'

She smiled very gently at the trembling girl and then she suddenly moved forward. Ellena noted vaguely that they were the same height, just as a kiss landed on her flushed cheek.

'Just let Ben sort it all out for you, my dear,' she whispered, and then she left them by themselves.

CHAPTER NINE

'Please sit down, and I'll get a drink,' Ben said curtly and disappeared.

Ellena looked around the room, still not quite sure why she was here. The room seemed rather crowded with furniture. A large, comfortable leather lounge suite was supplemented by several other large reclining chairs. A piano stood against one wall, and a large sound system against another. The top of the piano and several shelves of a large buffet were cluttered with ornaments and photographs.

Curiosity stirred her to take a couple of paces closer and peer at the photos. They were obviously mainly of family, all with that same dark Italian colouring. She was studying a photo of a much younger, laughing Ben when he came back carrying two large frosted glasses.

He paused as she turned guiltily away. 'Mamma is a compulsive collector of family photos.' He smiled as he presented her with a glass. 'It's just fruit juice,' he murmured as she hesitated.

'Th-thank you,' she said appreciatively.

He gestured to the lounge and she nervously sat down.

Ben took a long drink from his own glass, and then wiped his moustache between his fingers. She tore her eyes away and sipped at her own drink.

'I'm sorry about Mamma, Ellena. She's always on at me about finding a wife. Especially since my younger brother married a few months back.'

'Is. . .is that the one who's taken over the family business?'

His eyes narrowed slightly. 'Gossiping, Miss Provis?'

'No, no,' she said quickly. 'Mrs Davis talks about you sometimes.'

'Ah, yes, Mrs Davis. She was an acquaintance of my parents some years ago.'

'Was that before your father was killed in a car accident?' Ellena blurted out a little nervously.

A glint came into his dark eyes. 'A mine of information, our Mrs Davis,' he murmured. 'And what else did you find out about me, I wonder? That his death forced me to give up my full-time business administration course at university until recently to take charge of his business? That now I've just managed to finish it part-time, and very thankfully handed the business over to my brother, who knows a lot more about electronics than I ever will?'

Ellena was blushing painfully. 'No, I. . .that is. . .I had wondered if you were intending to stay on as the Macallister Complex's administrator when I heard about your own business,' she stammered, and took a deep breath and said in a firmer voice, 'Ben, I shouldn't be here. There's still so much to do at work.'

'Well, as far as I'm concerned this is all part of work,' he said grimly.

She hid her expression as she took another sip of the refreshing drink. Was work all they would ever be able to share?

'If Linda Terry hasn't upset you this morning, what has?'

Ben's tone was flat, almost expressionless. After a

moment, she looked up at him, her own face cool and withdrawn.

'It was a personal matter.'

His eyes narrowed, and then he put his drink down on the a small table near her and sat at the other end of the lounge.

'Ellena, are you in some kind of trouble with the law?' he asked very softly, his gaze fixed firmly on her.

'No!'

She stared at him. Horrified.

'Then why did a phone call from your solicitor upset you so much?'

She put a hand to her lips as she started to tremble. 'How. . .?'

'I answered the phone. He explained who he was before I transferred the call to the wards.'

'It's none of your business,' she said shakily.

'It is when it affects the DON of my best friend's rehabilitation complex the way it did!'

Suddenly he reached across and rescued her half-full glass from her nerveless fingers and put it down beside his. Then he sat back and turned his demanding gaze on her and waited.

After a moment, tears blinded her eyes again and she looked away.

'Solicitors also handle. . .handle the deceased's estates,' she said at long last in a choked voice.

He was very still for a moment. She was looking down at her hands clenched together when she heard him give a long-drawn-out sigh.

'So that was it,' she heard him mutter.

She sat there battling the tears again. She felt the sofa move and then he had gathered her up close against him until her head was once again on his shoulder.

'Do you think you could tell me about it?'

It was that same quiet voice she had heard when he'd thought he had found a dirty, untidy urchin in his DON's office an aeon ago. And suddenly she knew there was no one else she would rather tell.

'Was it your parents?' his voice murmured encouragingly.

'No, they were killed when I was thirteen. It. . .it was Gran. . .'

She choked for a moment. His arms tightened around her but he remained silent.

Falteringly she started to tell him about the wonderful woman who had been everything to her, who had looked after her as long as she could remember, even when her parents were alive but so wrapped up in their life together that there was little room for their daughter. She could still only bear to tell him briefly about those last few days in the coronary care unit, about the dreadful time that had followed.

'There are only a few distant cousins left up in the area now. I even met one of them for the very first time when Gran was in hospital,' she said sadly at last.

'And the phone call today?'

'The old farm has to be sold. He rang to say someone had made an offer for it,' she said in a constricted voice.

Just saying it out loud brought the reality of it all home again, and the tears once more trickled down her cheeks.

'But I don't quite understand,' Ben said thoughtfully, 'why nobody, not even Chris, ever mentioned just why you took your holidays when you did.'

The tears continued to fall as she mumbled in a choked voice, 'Because when I. . .when I rang Matthew it. . .it had just happened, and I just couldn't. . .couldn't put it into words. I was overdue for holidays, and. . .and. . .'

The tears had become a torrent as she heard his murmur, 'And today's the first time you've really cried.'

It was more statement than question, and suddenly she knew he was right. Oh, there had been tears at the funeral, even afterwards when she had packed those African violets so carefully into the car, knowing Gran would never be able to croon over their beauty again. But not until today had she really grieved for the loss of her old home, her youth. She had kept herself busy doing what had to be done, almost as though it was all happening to someone else. To a stranger. Even the long hours she had worked sorting out Macallister's had been almost welcomed, a panacea for pain.

She didn't know how long he held her as she cried again. But when the anguish at last subsided she realised he had somehow pulled her on to his knee and tucked her against his chest, letting all the pain pour out of her until she was drained. He had even released her topknot so that he could rest her head under his chin. One of his brown hands gently massaged her scalp and ran through her long silken tresses, while his soft voice soothed and comforted her as though she were a child.

After a while, she gave a deep sigh and went to sit up.

'I. . .I'm sorry. . .' she whispered, and then subsided again as he muttered something indistinguishable against her hair and pulled her back into his arms.

A quiver pierced through her. He must have felt it too, because for a moment she felt his body tense, and suddenly there was a different atmosphere between them. She was aware that one of his hands was brushing against her breast. Heat swept through her. His hand moved and she felt him give a soft groan as he cupped the fullness of her breast in his hand.

'So beautiful,' he breathed, 'so very beautiful.'

She held her breath as his fingers found her nipple through her clothes and gently fondled it. It was as though her body began to waken from a long sleep. Suddenly the other breast felt cold, neglected. Then it too was being touched. Caressed. And still it wasn't enough.

There was another soft moan and this time she was vaguely aware that it had come from her own lips the moment before he possessed them with his own. And then there was only that wonderful electric current sweeping her from head to toe.

His fingers fumbled at her blouse, and she heard his hiss of frustration when he realised there were no buttons to undo and then he had pulled it from the waistband, and with a sigh of relief she felt his trembling fingers reaching underneath, slipping inside her lace bra, touching her flesh, kneading, massaging, while the flame grew hotter and hotter.

'Oh, my darling, darling girl. I've been so hungry for the touch of you, the taste of you. You've been driving me mad.'

His lips moved to her swollen eyes, her cheeks, nibbled at her neck and then they were on her lips again, probing inside, seeking out her sweetness. One hand had moved down to her thigh and was ever so gently stroking higher and higher up under her skirt.

She tensed as his fingers found their goal.

He stilled. Then he raised his face and she looked at him from dazed eyes.

Suddenly his face lost colour. She watched him close his eyes tightly and swallow convulsively. Then his hands were gone from her body and she bounced bonelessly for a moment as he sprang up from the sofa as though stung.

'Oh, no!' she heard him groan. 'What have I done?'

Her breath caught in her throat and then she too was standing on legs that barely supported her. She staggered, and his hands came out and gripped her shoulders. For one heavenly moment she thought he went to pull her into his arms again, but then he pushed her further away and when she was steady again his hands dropped to his sides. And there was only the quick rise and fall of their shattered breathing as they stared at each other.

Then Ben ran a hand through his hair with an agitated movement.

'Oh, Ellie, Ellie! Now is *not* the time for this!' His voice was harsh and low. His eyes dropped to her dishevelled clothing and he swallowed again and said faintly, 'You'd—better. . .'

Ellena felt her face flame. She looked down and saw that her blouse was still pushed askew and there was a large expanse of flesh still on view that had been released from her bra.

She gasped and turned her back on him, her trembling fingers working desperately to restore order. When her blouse was at last safely tucked away again into her skirt, she just stood there with her back to him, desperately trying to think.

'I'm dreadfully sorry. . .Ellena. That wasn't supposed to happen. At least not yet,' she thought she heard him mutter.

She stiffened. He sounded as shaken as she did, and for some reason that boosted her own self-confidence. She turned slowly around to find that he had moved several paces away and was standing very stiffly with his back to her and his hands clenched beside him.

'Not yet? What. . .what do you mean?'

He didn't move.

She took a step closer to him, and said a lot louder, 'Was that never supposed to happen, or was this just the wrong. . .' she gulped breathlessly '. . .the wrong time?'

At that he swung around so violently, she actually flinched. But then she tilted her chin and stood her ground.

There was no way she would be ashamed of her response to him. She loved him. Even if that had only been for him the emotion of the moment. Or his masculine hormones stirring. Whatever his reason, she had kissed him back and revelled in his lovemaking. . . simply because she loved him.

'There are things you don't know about. But now is definitely not the right time,' he ground out.

Ellena's burst of confidence dissolved like a pricked balloon.

'Linda,' she said flatly, and dropped her eyes so he wouldn't see the pain that ripped through her. 'So you're the type of man who can. . .can kiss me like that while you are taking out Linda.'

He was still. 'Linda? I've never dated Linda.' His voice sounded faintly puzzled, but then became tinged with remembered anger as he added strongly, 'And

I haven't the faintest idea why you called her my girlfriend before.'

She looked swiftly at him, and he suddenly reached out and grasped her above the elbows. 'But we've got to talk about her. Ellie, she musn't know, but——' his voice was urgent, and, as though on cue, the phone shrilled out its summons.

Ellena jumped, but Ben didn't move, just stared at her from dark molten eyes.

'Hadn't you better answer that?' she murmured at last.

He moved jerkily then, and snatched the phone. 'Yes?' he barked. He listened for a moment, and then looked up at her with a worried frown. 'Just a moment, Miss Provis is right here. It's Joan Wheat,' he added to Ellena, and held out the receiver.

Her hand shook as she snatched at it.

'Ellena? Thank goodness you're there! It's Mrs Davis. She's collapsed. Looks like another CVA. I thought you'd want to know.'

Ellena closed her eyes tightly, but the deep groan was inward. Outwardly, her professional training took over, as she snapped out a couple of questions.

And then, after listening intently, she said very quietly, 'Thanks, Joan, I'll be there as soon as possible.'

Ben was beside her when she replaced the phone.

In answer to his raised eyebrows, she said urgently, 'We've got to get back. It's Mrs Davis.'

She headed for the door, but Ben's hand shot out and grabbed her arm. 'Not like that. You're a mess. The bathroom's this way.'

He started pulling her in the other direction. She resisted for a moment, and then realised the sense of not returning looking as though she had been. . .been thoroughly kissed!

Silently, almost impersonally Ben shoved her into the bathroom, pulled out a drawer and supplied brush and comb, before disappearing to return with a towel.

'You can put on a bit of make-up in the car on the way,' he said crisply.

And this she found herself doing a few minutes later. It wasn't until she sat back after dabbing on a touch of powder and lipstick that Ben spoke again.

'What did Joan say?'

'Mrs Davis collapsed when she was being walked,' Ellena said after a moment in a tight voice. 'They managed to get her back to bed and start oxygen. Fortunately James Gill arrived before they could even ring him. Joan said it was still too late. There. . .there wasn't much he could do.'

And so a grim-faced Dr Gill confirmed when they reached the ward.

'Massive cerebro-vascular accident,' he told them abruptly. 'And where on earth were you, Miss Provis?' he asked accusingly. 'None of the staff seemed to have a clue where you were!'

Joan Wheat was quietly talking on the phone, but she looked up sharply at the harsh tones.

'Now, just a moment,' Ben snapped before Ellena could respond, 'I told Sister Terry myself that Miss Provis was leaving early to go home. She wasn't well, so I took her to my place first on the way.'

'Hmmph!' snorted Dr Gill. 'Then why on earth didn't that. . .that da. . .that woman say so?'

'Yes, I agree,' said Joan through her teeth, as she put the phone down. 'When you didn't come in answer to the emergency buzzer, I had one of the girls searching everywhere for you both. It was Miss Burgess who eventually told us she saw you driving off somewhere.'

'Let's not worry about that now,' Ben said firmly.

'Did you get on to the family?' Ellena snapped after giving him a brief glare.

'I haven't been able to reach the daughter, but that was a grandson in Sydney who said he'd ring his father at work.'

They all looked up as the sound of high heels clipped towards them along the corridor.

'Oh, no,' groaned Joan under her breath.

They were all frozen as Mrs Davis's daughter paused near them.

'Good. . .good morning,' the woman said nervously as she looked from one to the other. 'I know it's not visiting hours, but I told Mother I'd bring her back her washing this morning because the girls have netball practice after school so I——'

'Mrs Grey,' interrupted Ellena gently, 'would you please come with us for a moment? I'm afraid Dr Gill and I have something to tell you.'

It was a long time later before Ellena was at last free to close her office door behind her, slump down on her chair and rest her head on her hands.

After a few moments the door opened again, and without looking up, she knew it was Ben.

'Have you eaten yet?' he asked in a concerned voice.

She shook her head slightly and then was still again.

'I thought not.'

Something was placed on the table in front of her, and she at last opened her eyes as the smell of coffee reached her. The tray was very daintily prepared. A

small appetising salad and a small dish of sweets were
so tempting that she suddenly realised how hungry she
was. Still resting her forehead on one hand, she looked
up at him sadly.

'Are you all right?' he asked in concern. You're
very white.'

'Yes,' she said wearily, 'I've just never learnt to be
as detached as I should be when something like this
happens.'

'No, you wouldn't.' His voice was very gentle and
there was a tender look on his face.

'Oh, I know what I told Mrs Grey was true,' Ellena
suddenly appealed to him, 'Mrs Davis absolutely hated
not being able to go back to her own home, hated
being so dependent on others, and so perhaps it's all
for the best. But I can't help wondering if Linda may
have been right this time. Mrs Davis wasn't fit enough
to do as much as we tried to get her to.'

'I had several long talks with that wonderful old lady
in the weeks I've been here,' Ben said slowly. 'She
had a mountain of yarns about the local coalmining
history. Her family were heavily involved in the indus-
try. She even said to me once that she would much
rather not have survived her stroke if she couldn't go
home. And she's been so much happier since you
coaxed her back to her old self. Above all, you were
giving her back her dignity and control over her
life again.'

His sudden smile at her was unexpectedly sweet and
full of understanding. A fiery dart of love shot through
her veins, blurring her eyes for a moment so she could
not see. She moved suddenly, clenching her hands in
her lap and looking down at them, hoping she had not
given herself away as he continued in a soft voice.

'She thought the world of you. Even though you did have to fight that battle royal to stop her sleeping so much during the day, and persuading her to sleep at night without her precious tablets. She preferred it this way. I'm sure of that. Giving up as she had was far, far worse for someone of her personality and background.'

He reached out and ran the back of a finger tenderly over her cheek and then over the hand her head was resting on. Then she felt him lift a strand of her hair and gently tuck it behind her ear. The finger continued its feather touch soothingly across her face. She quivered helplessly, physically unable to utter a word, longing to reach out to him but not daring to after his rejection of her.

She heard his voice deepen as he said softly, 'Do you have to stay on duty? Couldn't you go home early just for once? I'm sure the staff can cope now.'

Ellena kept her eyes tightly closed for a moment, savouring his touch. Then she exercised every last scrap of self-will and pulled away. Listlessly she stared at the food in front of her and then reached over to pick up a piece of cheese and pop it into her mouth with her fingers.

'I was hoping to sort out the next fortnight's roster before the weekend,' she said a little stiffly.

Without consciously thinking about it, she picked up a fork and speared a small piece of sliced lamb.

'That's a job that Julie usually did,' she added, and then looked up at him appealingly. 'Were there any applications in the mail today for the deputy's job?'

Ben hesitated, and then nodded. 'One firm application, and a couple of phone call enquiries. But that can wait until Monday. There may be more from tomorrow's advertisement. Now look,' he added hastily as she went to speak, 'don't worry about that right now. I've already promised we'll get you some help as soon as we can. What we've got to worry about now is making sure the DON doesn't get sick from too many long hours! How soon do you think you could be finished up here? Half an hour?'

And suddenly Ellena knew he was right. She was absolutely exhausted, both physically and emotionally. Too tired to even eat any more of the food in front of her. Too tired to be able to survive long in this man's presence without begging him to again wrap her in his arms and comfort and love her.

She pushed back her chair and stood up decisively. 'You're perfectly right! I'm going this minute.'

'Without even drinking your coffee?' His voice was whimsical as he stared down at the hardly touched tray, and then he looked ruefully up at her. 'I made that myself.'

Ellena wanted nothing more at that moment than to walk into his arms and have him hold her. But all she could do was weakly reach for the coffee. It had cooled while they talked, and with a few swallows it was gone.

'There,' she said as calmly as she could, 'all done.'

Still without looking at him, she picked up the phone with a trembling hand. While she was waiting for someone on the ward to answer so she could tell them she was leaving, Ben picked up the tray and walked out. His back was rigid, and she knew somehow he was upset with her. Only as she heard a rather breathless voice answer the phone did she realise she hadn't even said thank you for his offering.

A few minutes later, Ellena was driving out of the car park. She noted with interest that there was a car in the driveway of the Hansens' residence. Her foot eased on the accelerator for a moment, tempted to see if they were home, but she knew she was too emotionally wrought-up, too exhausted, too tired for explanations, and continued on her way. There would be time enough on Monday. Perhaps even if she went in for a few hours tomorrow. . .

But there was another phone call late that afternoon. The businessman from Sydney was travelling up to the farm again to take other members of his family to have a look. Very reluctantly, Ellena agreed to meet them there.

It was late when she arrived home Saturday evening with a much lighter heart about the future of the home she loved. The family had been delightful. Far from being hobby farmers, they were simply tired of the rush and turmoil of the city.

'Both our parents had farms in the Hunter Valley when we were kids,' Ken Woods had said as they admired the blossoms on a very old, pink flowering peach tree in the neglected garden. And then added ruefully, 'We know we've a lot to learn about farming ahead of us. But at least our knowledge of business practices will be handy.'

He had gone on to explain enthusiastically that they were employing a manager for his business in Sydney and, no doubt because of her rather doubtful expression, had assured Ellena with a twinkle that there would still be plenty of money for capital to put into farming.

They had been brimming over with ideas. Were even seriously researching the possibility of turning some of the land into a vineyard as many had in suitable areas of the Hunter Valley. As she had accompanied them

over the farm, she had been captivated by his obvious
love for the country. Fortunately his wife also shared
his enthusiasm. Their teenage children obviously
weren't quite so sure, and she hoped fervently that it
would work out for them all.

There had been healing for Ellena as she had walked
over the green paddocks and down to the sparkling
little creek. A chortling kookaburra in a tall gum tree
had laughed at them, and Ellena had found herself
laughing too. And there had been plenty of time to
think on the long drive home

As she prepared for bed, it was as though a great
burden had rolled from her. Suddenly it was easier to
feel more optimistic that everything would work out
at Macallister's. And with Ben, too.

She paused and frowned. Linda had definitely indicated several times that she had been out with Ben.
Other nurses had even muttered that he was far too
good for her. But he had denied it. And he had never
given her the impression he was the kind of man who
would deny such a thing if it was not so.

But what had Linda hoped to gain? Exactly what she
had, Ellena suddenly acknowledged grimly. A sister in
a relationship with the administrator would make the
DON think twice before reprimanding her. Especially
when relations between the two in admin were already
so shaky.

But even as she scowled at realising how gullible she
had been, her heart lifted. Suddenly her love for that
infuriating, complex man, Ben Nicoletti, didn't seem
quite so hopeless. He had been so wonderful to her
yesterday. . .

As she drifted off to sleep, it was with the memory
of his lips on hers, the naked, raw emotion in his eyes

until he had remembered Linda. Despite his rejection, hope suddenly surged that there just could be a chance. . .a chance he would perhaps one day return her love. One day. . .

It was late when she woke on Sunday morning. For the first time in those long, painful weeks, she stretched luxuriously with a sense of wellbeing. The day before had been a real release from the tension of work and the uncertainty of the farm, and she knew she had much to be thankful for.

She glanced at her watch. The service she usually went to at the local church started in half an hour. She could make it if she rushed. Then decided, no, she felt too comfortably relaxed and lazy.

Her thoughts flew to Ben, wondering with a faint smile if he too would be at church this morning. She never had thought to ask him where he worshipped, only that apparently he rarely missed. She wondered briefly if Linda ever felt the need to go to church.

A frown crossed her forehead. A calm, dignified Linda had denied seeing her in the car with Ben, denied knowing that she was going home, and there had been no time to tell Ben about that, no chance to follow it up. Truly, that woman seemed more than merely irrational at times. Surely she must have known that Ben himself would say he himself had told her. And that would give the DON reason alone to ask for her resignation, or even to terminate her employment.

Then she determinedly put thoughts of work from her mind. Yesterday's weather had been perfect, and the forecast had been for another such day. For this one day she would try and relax, and perhaps tomorrow she would be able to tackle all her problems with a fresh mind.

Slowly she stretched again and looked at the stream of sun coming through her window.

Too lovely a day to stay indoors.

And she really did feel the need to be with other people, the need to be in God's house just to feel closer to Gran who had been a devout believer all her life, the need to say thank you and to worship.

She thought for a moment, and then sprang out of bed. There was another church in the next suburb whose service time started much later.

It was still a bit of a rush, but the congregation of the large church was just rising to sing the first hymn as Ellena was ushered to a seat at one side.

As always, faith was stirred, hope rekindled, and she turned after the benediction to leave with a deep sense of peace and certainty that she was not alone, that her life would always be in safe hands.

And came face to face with Ben.

'Why, Ben! So this is where——'

The words broke off.

It was a scowling, pale-faced, incredibly grim Ben. He nodded abruptly and started to brush past her without a word. Linda was behind him, and simply stared triumphantly and coldly at her before following Ben.

Ellena's delighted smile was left frozen on her face, and a heavy stone slowly filled the space where her heart had for a moment throbbed with joy.

CHAPTER TEN

MONDAY morning was a direct contrast to the beautiful weather of the weekend. Very strong gusts of wind coming off the lake forced Ellena to decide against using her umbrella as protection against the driving rain as she ran across the car park at Macallister's.

The temperature had dropped dramatically as winter had one more fling trying to stop the birth of the blossoms and leaves of spring. It was a relief to reach the quietness and the warmth of the front foyer as she paused to take off her dripping plastic raincoat and hat. She'd had very little sleep and had decided she might as well be at work than at home where she had too much time to think. So the day staff still had not arrived as she at last hurried to her office. There was much to be sorted out today, and the first thing she tackled calmly was the roster.

Fortunately, for once there were only a few requests for special days off, and she was able to finish without too much difficulty the rough draft to be checked later. The patients were being moved out of the dining-room, and the office staff still had not arrived when Ellena took a deep breath and moved to the table that held her typewriter.

It didn't take her long to type the few lines, then she decisively pulled the typed sheet of paper from the machine and read it through again sadly. Here was the death of her dreams.

She had just sealed it in an envelope and was writing

on the front when someone rapped on the door and then turned the door handle at the same time. As the man put his head around the corner, she was tensing herself to see Ben. Instead, to her absolute delight, it was Chris Hansen.

'So it was your car in the car park,' his deep voice said as she sprang to her feet.

She was around the desk and striding towards him before she realised how cool the tone of his voice had been and how he was frowning at her. He ignored the hand she thrust out towards him.

'Chris, I'm so pleased you're back,' she faltered, as he just stood there studying her face as though she were a stranger.

'Are you?' The sarcasm in his voice brought her head up.

'Yes, of course I am,' she said hesitantly. 'Why on earth shouldn't I be? There's a lot for you to catch up on.'

'So I believe,' he said slowly, still studying her face.

'Is Jean with you?'

His face softened as it always did when he thought of his wife. 'We returned on Friday,' he said briefly. 'Peggy and George too.' Then his expression darkened again and he added sternly, 'But you had already disappeared—again, I might add—when we came over to say hello and see how things were going. Need I say we were appalled, absolutely appalled by what's been happening in our absence! We didn't dream Julie wouldn't be back from sick leave in a few days!'

Her heart sank. 'Then. . .then you saw Ben.'

'No, not yet. He too had gone out early on business, and already gone to Sydney when we contacted his mother on Saturday morning. We also tried to contact you, but you had gone away again.' His scowl grew blacker. 'And why on earth did you go home so early on Friday, the way you did, and leave the staff here to cope alone after the death of one our long-term patients?'

Of all the things he could have said to her, that was the last thing she had thought of. She stared at him in absolute amazement. 'What on earth do you mean? I did *not* leave the staff to cope alone. In fact there was absolutely nothing more to be done for Mrs Davis or her family when I went off duty.'

For a moment he looked uncertain. 'But I understood you didn't even stay to speak to her son when he arrived.'

'He didn't indicate in any way when I spoke to him on the phone that he wished to speak to me any further when he came to pick up Mrs Davis's belongings. Mrs Grey had been too upset to bother about that,' Ellena said stiffly. 'I knew the staff on duty would have them all ready. I still see no reason why I should have been expected to wait for two to three hours for him to get here!'

'Two to—oh!' Chris ran his hand suddenly through his hair. 'Of course. He lived in Sydney,' he said abruptly.

Hurt shot through Ellena. 'I thought after the time I've worked for you, you'd know me well enough to be sure I wouldn't leave until everything was sorted out.' Ellena had to ask, but she was sure she already knew the answer when she added angrily, 'I take it you arrived after Sister Wheat had gone off duty, and it was Linda Terry you spoke to?'

Before Chris could answer, they heard Ben's voice

outside calling out a greeting to one of the patients. The look of relief on Chris's face was echoed in Ellena's as a moment later he appeared in the doorway.

'Buddy! I thought you might be over early!' Ben beamed with delight as he pumped Chris's hand and then gave him a huge hug. 'Oh, man! Am I glad to see you!' he added fervently.

'Ready to give up being administrator of this little place already, are we?' Chris mocked affectionately as he tolerated his friend's exuberance.

'This "little" place is twice as much work as our whole family business!' Ben laughed grimly. 'But I'm still thinking seriously about staying on. . .if. . .'

Only Chris noted the uncertainty in his friend's expression as he paused and looked across at Ellena. She had moved abruptly away as Chris started to speak, but swung back as their words penetrated. She had assumed that Ben's position as administrator was a permanent one. But did this mean he might leave? Was she throwing away her job for nothing?

Suddenly she realised how very little she really knew about the man she loved. She only knew that the mere sight of him still had the power to make her shake inside and confirm that she was about to do the right thing. As she had decided in the darkest hours of the night, there was no way she could work here day after day in such close proximity to him and leave herself open to such deep hurt.

She drew a deep breath as Ben looked across the room at her, and all the pleasure and laughter fled from his expression.

'Good morning, Ellena,' he said very quietly.

'Good morning,' she managed to say distantly.

He hesitated, and Ellena was aware that Chris's gaze

had sharpened as he looked quickly from one to the other.

'I hope you enjoyed the service Sunday morning?' Ben said quietly without taking his eyes from hers.

An expression filled their black depths then that made Ellena's foolish heart leap. Then it settled again as she remembered the way he had ignored her, the way Linda Terry had reached to hold his hand as though it was her right. The way she had tossed and turned far into the night.

She raised her head proudly. 'As a matter of fact, I was greatly blessed and helped by the service.'

And she spoke nothing but the truth. She still wasn't sure how she could have come to work today if there had not been the refuge of prayer and faith that had sustained her since then.

Something like pain flashed across Ben's face and colour tinted his cheeks. He swallowed, and then Chris Hansen's quietly authoritative voice cut in.

'We'll spend some time together later, Ellena. First, I want to have a talk with Ben. I can see more has been happening here than I've already been told.'

'Already been told? Then you've been here a while?' Ben murmured, not taking his eyes from Ellena until Chris spoke again.

'I spent some time here late Friday.'

Ben's eyes flashed to Chris and then back again to Ellena. They lit up momentarily as he exclaimed ruefully, 'Uh-oh! Then it sounds as if you spoke to our Sister Terry! Whatever she said, I'm sure she's managed to twist it somehow.'

Ellena stared at Ben. Suddenly she was confused once again. Ben had never impressed her as the sort of person who would speak so derogatorily about anyone, especially. . .

The men turned to leave, and Ellena suddenly remembered.

'Chr—Dr Hansen,' she called sharply, 'I may as well give this to you straight away,' and picked up the envelope from the desk.

Her resignation.

He glanced at it as she thrust it into his hand, murmured a curt, 'Thank you,' before striding after Ben.

The door closed behind them.

She stared blindly in front of her. Then her eyes closed and she drew a painful, shuddering breath.

Oh, God, have I done the right thing?

Then she forced herself to move. Stiffly. Back to her desk. Exercising the rigid self-control she had realised some time during those long hours of the night would be essential today. . .to do her work properly.

She picked up the notebook and folder she always took with her and deliberately tried to cut off thoughts of anything and anyone except the patients and problems she would meet on her usual round.

Then another knife-thrust. How many more days would she have to care for the patients?

There had been several other excellent applicants for this position over twelve months ago, and no doubt there would still be several of them who would apply again.

Determinedly she thrust that thought away, and there was only a polite smile on her face as she greeted the RN in charge, a woman employed only during the last couple of weeks. Fortunately Linda was on afternoon shift.

'Good morning, Sister Stacy. I know you're busy,

and Dr Hansen's back and will no doubt be doing a thorough round later on this morning, so just tell me anything new that's happened over the weekend, and then I'll just quickly see the patients by myself.'

Nothing seemed to have occurred very much out of the usual. Sam Macgregor was managing much better putting on and taking off his artificial leg independently. So well, in fact in his walking frame, that he would soon be progressing to just a walking stick, and would not be long before he could be discharged. Ellena made a note to remind Chris about an OT home assessment for any alterations to the house to help him cope there.

There was little to report on the weekly routine observations except that one of the CVAs who was obese and supposed to be losing weight on a special diet had unexpectedly put on a couple of kilograms.

'Family been in much last week?' Ellena asked thoughtfully.

'Well, yes,' Helen Stacy said hesitantly, 'but we mentioned that to the staff and they don't think they brought in any sweets or anything except diet soft drink. But his anti-depressant medication was changed by Dr Gill last week.'

'Could be drug-induced fluid retention, I suppose,' Ellena sighed. 'Let's hope not; he's been much brighter on Tolvon. He'd better go on a daily weigh for a while, and keep a close eye on him during visitors in case they are slipping him extra food. Far too many well-meaning people think we're starving patients when they see them losing weight the way he's been.'

They discussed the progress of a few others, and when they reached Mr Dredge Ellena said, 'I thought he was making real progress last week since the gradual

change from Sinemet to Symmetrel. He was certainly
walking better with less catching of his feet. It's
amazing. Most patients do better on the Sinemet
but it just made him too nauseous. Could be of
course that he wasn't taking all his doses. Appetite
improving still?'

'He seemed all right yesterday,' Helen agreed.

Something in her voice made Ellena look up at her
quickly.

Helen shrugged. 'Oh, there's nothing I can really
put my finger on this morning. He hasn't slept as well
the past three nights, the night staff reported. But it
was hot, and he complained more than usual about his
feet burning once he was in bed. And there's nothing
unusual about that with Parkinson's. And he certainly
doesn't complain of nausea any more. His tremor may
be very slightly worse, but then that often varies from
day to day. He's probably just tired.'

'Probably,' Ellena said slowly.

Helen Stacy was a good nurse, and Ellena had learnt
over the years to listen when someone like her sensed
there was something wrong, even when she wasn't
sure why.

So the first person she went to see was Mr Dredge.
She had become very fond of him and his wife. It had
only been a couple of days after she met them that he
had insisted Ellena call them by their first names. She
had wondered at the time if he knew that one of the
Hansens' rules for the staff was that they were only
permitted to call patients by their first names after
being given permission to do so.

Never once had they mentioned again that they knew
the Hansens, and Ellena had not thought it necessary
to tell anyone what had obviously been a slip of the

tongue on that first anxious day. Their son was also a reserved, pleasant man, very unlike his wife, who had never visited him that Ellena was aware of until the previous Friday.

The memory of Miss Burgess and that dreadful day made her wince. Thrusting all truant thoughts of Ben firmly aside, she smiled at the old man when she found him resting on a side patio. The wind and rain had stopped and weak sun was trying to push past a few hovering dark clouds.

'Good morning, John,' she teased him gently, 'sneaking a bit of fresh air before Lorraine starts her fun and games, are you?'

She grinned back at him when he scowled at her.

Lorraine was the very keen diversional therapist who worked from nine until lunchtime each day. Many of the old people were quite content to just sit and watch television all day in between their therapy sessions, but Monday to Friday Chris had banned the TV until the midday show came on, declaring they watched too much the rest of the time as it was.

Only at weekends were they allowed a rest from Lorraine's exuberant efforts to stimulate them mentally as well as physically with a variety of crafts, games and entertainment. George Macallister had often joined her to egg on the faint at heart or to assist the handicapped despite his own hemiplegia from his first stroke over two years before.

Now John said belligerently, 'I'm playing cards with Sam whether she likes it or not!'

Ellena kept the smile on her face, but she studied him carefully as she chatted away to him for a few minutes. He was certainly far more tense than she remembered seeing him for a long time.

'See the family over the weekend?' she asked lightly at last.

He sat up jerkily. 'Lady Burgess was here Friday,' he snarled.

Ellena knew how much he disliked his daughter-in-law but she tensed at the violence of his response. Then he lifted a hand from the arm of his chair, and to Ellena's dismay it started to shake quite violently.

'That. . .that damned woman! What Tim ever saw in her I'll never know!' he exploded in a shaking voice.

Ellena reached across swiftly and grabbed his hand.

'Hey, calm down, John,' she said with alarm.

'You should have heard what she said about. . . about that. . .that poor woman. . .the one that died. . .and you. . .and you. . .she. . .she. . .said should have been in. . .in a nursing home. . .said I. . .I. . .should. . .should. . .'

By this time, beads of perspiration were beginning to collect on his forehead as his breath became deep and laboured, his voice more and more indistinct. Then his whole body became rigid and started to shake.

Ellena moved swiftly.

She rushed to an alarm button just inside on the hallway and pressed it three times, and then she was back with the now violently shaking man.

Ellena was trying to prevent his rigid, shaking body from sliding out of his chair when Ann White rushed towards them.

'Get Sister, and then Dr Hansen stat. Tell them Parkinsonian crisis,' she rapped out.

Helen must have met the EN on the way and arrived a few moments later with a wheelchair. They had somehow managed to get the frail body on to the chair and started wheeling him along the corridor when Chris and Ben arrived.

'IV phenobarb, Ellena,' snapped Chris as he reached them, 'Nurse is getting the oxygen ready. Ben, take over from Sister.'

Ellena waited until Chris had taken her place trying to keep the violently shaking man on the chair and raced to the dangerous drug cupboard. Helen quickly followed her to the treatment-room, handed her the DD cupboard keys and grabbed the IV tray.

'I'll check the drugs with you later,' she said hurriedly before disappearing again.

The phenobarbitone sodium ampoules were not in their usual place. Ellena bit her lip as she searched hurriedly, hardly believing there wasn't any until at last she grabbed the DD book. There it was in Linda's untidy scrawl.

'Returned to pharmacy.'

She swiftly checked the index for another sedative. The strongest benzodiazepine in injection form still stocked was diazepam. She hesitated a moment then grabbed a couple of ampoules, relocked the cupboard and raced back to Mr Dredge's room.

They had just managed to lift him on to the bed. The EN was slipping on an oxygen mask, Ben was taking off Mr Dredge's lace-up shoes, and Chris was just slipping the tourniquet around his upper arm.

'Sorry, Dr Hansen, no phenobarb. Valium do?' she gasped.

Helen looked at her sharply as she tore open a syringe packet and dropped it on to the tray.

Chris scowled as he reached for the syringe and fitted on a cannula. 'It'll have to, won't it! What strength?'

'Five milligrams,' Ellena said in a choked voice.

She had always worked exceptionally well with Chris Hansen, and been very friendly with Jean, and now his attitude cut deeply.

'We'll probably need at least two for now.' He glared at her. 'You'd better get another one.'

'I brought two.'

'Good! Have them ready,' he snapped as he bent over his patient.

There was silence for a moment as the needle searched for and found a vein. A few drops of dark blood was drawn into the syringe. He quickly took it off the cannula. Ellena handed him the small tray with another syringe already filled with the drug she had drawn up after Helen had double-checked the ampoules.

He silently checked the writing on the ampoules as she routinely held them for him to look at also, and then he slowly commenced to inject into the cannula in Mr Dredge's arm.

'I left instructions for Dr Gill to change his medication. What's he on?'

Helen answered crisply, explaining the change ordered over a week ago.

'Hmm, he should be stabilised on that now. Any emotional upset recently? This morning even?'

'Yes,' said Ellena.

She felt Ben's gaze switch from watching Chris to her face, and looked helplessly across the bed at him.

'We lost a patient Friday, Chris,' Ben said softly, his eyes sympathetic and warm as he stared at her.

Chris had paused after giving about half the contents in the syringe. His fingers were feeling the racing pulse and waiting for the drug to take effect. He glanced up sharply at Ben, and then followed his gaze across the bed.

After a brief moment Chris asked quietly, 'I know, but how did that affect John?'

'Mrs Davis collapsed while she was being walked right past him,' Ellena said in an undertone.

Chris looked away, and there was silence again as they watched the rigid figure on the bed slowly relaxing. His shaking was still severe but not as violent.

'But that was three days ago,' Chris said as he bent to insert a little more of the calming sedation.

'But. . .I don't think it was her death as much as. . . as. . .' Ellena paused, wondering how best to word her concern with both the EN and RN present.

'John also was very upset after a visit from his daughter-in-law on Friday morning,' Ben said quickly, 'I spoke to him that afternoon.'

Ellena looked back at him with surprise. She hadn't been told about any upset. Then she realised Annabel Burgess must have visited her father-in-law immediately after their encounter at the front entrance. The woman was certainly quite capable of taking her anger out on an old man.

Heat flooded through her as the memories came flooding back of what had happened later that morning at Ben's home.

By the expression that changed Ben's eyes to black molten depths as he looked intently at her, he too was remembering.

Neither saw the quick look Chris gave them both again before he muttered, 'Well, well!'

They looked at him, and he added quickly, 'There, that's settling him down.'

Before he could say any more, Ellena rushed to

confess very softly, hating to have this conversation in case the old man could hear them, 'A few minutes ago I asked Mr Dredge if he'd seen any of his family over the weekend, and he mentioned his daughter-in-law. That. . .that was when he became very upset.'

'But I've been a little concerned about him over the weekend,' Helen said quietly. 'That's why Miss Provis had gone to speak to him.'

Ellena threw her a grateful look as Chris straightened at last after administering the last of the valium.

'Well, he's settling now. Half-hourly obs, please, Sister. I'll leave the cannula in for a few hours and keep the oxygen going a while longer. We'll increase the Symmetrel for a few days, and then review it. Let me know immediately if the tachycardia returns. Oh, and don't worry about contacting his wife, I'll do that myself.'

It would be wonderful to have a doctor next door again, thought Ellena thankfully as Chris strode from the room. Helen followed him as Ellena finished putting a bung on the cannula. She started to tear off some plaster to firmly strap down the cannula to the arm, when she realised that Ben had paused instead of following Chris. Trying desperately to ignore him, she efficiently finished what she was doing and reached for an op-site dressing.

'Miss Provis, we need to sit down with Dr Hansen as soon as possible and sort a few things out,' Ben said in a controlled voice. 'He said he had to do a full ward round as soon as Dr Gill gets here this morning. But would some time this afternoon be convenient?'

She kept her face averted as she applied the dressing, and then started clearing away the IV tray for Helen, wondering desperately if he knew yet about her resignation.

'I would very much appreciate the opportunity to clear everything up!' Ellena said grimly at last. 'The sooner, the better! But the first thing I need to do is find out why certain DDs are no longer being stocked.'

'No! The first thing we need to find out is why Dr Hansen believes you told him yourself there was no way you would forfeit your annual leave to return to help with the staff crisis here at Macallister's!'

The used IV tray nearly slipped out of Ellena's hands as she swung around.

'I what?' she gasped.

'He had just finished telling me when the alarm went off,' Ben said very calmly in a low voice, completely ignoring Ann White still taking Mr Dredge's blood-pressure. 'He insists that he rang you himself the day Matthew collapsed, apparently only a couple of days after you had been given permission for further leave. He was utterly dumbfounded and bitterly disappointed in you. He insists you were incredibly rude to him, even saying he was crazy to expect you to do anything of the sort as give up your precious holiday!'

CHAPTER ELEVEN

'No! THAT's not possible! I never. . .' Ellena gasped, but her voice faded away as Ben's deep eyes seemed to pierce to the very heart of her.

'That's why we need to see you as soon as possible,' he said very softly, and then turned on his heel and was gone.

Ellena swayed for a moment. Chris had rung her? Chris had spoken to her? When? How? And did Ben believe too that. . .that. . .?

'Miss Provis?' the timid voice of the EN intruded on her anguish and bewilderment.

Ellena had taken a step forward, the IV tray clutched tightly in both hands. She paused and stared blankly at the young, round-eyed girl.

'The. . .the DD book,' Ann faltered and pointed.

Only then did Ellena realise she had left that important book on the bed table. She snatched it up with a choked word of thanks and walked slowly out of the room.

She went into the treatment-room, placed the tray on a bench, and stared blindly in front of her. The day that Matthew had collapsed, she had realised some time ago, was the day of Gran's funeral. There had been no phone call that she could remember. Surely even in the state she had been in she would never. . . never. . .

She shuddered.

'Miss Provis, are you all right for me to check the drugs with you? Miss Provis. . .?'

'Er. . .yes. Of course. The diazepam.' Ellena fumbled with the book and somehow found the right page.

'If I could have the keys?'

With a tremendous effort, Ellena pulled herself together. She handed the drug cupboard keys over to Helen Stacy and wrote up the book while the RN lifted out the rest of the diazepam ampoules and then watched as she counted them. They both signed the book, and as Helen went to close the cupboard, Ellena stopped her.

'I can't understand why there are so few sedations still stocked, Helen. Do you know anything about it?'

'No, not really,' Helen said hesitantly, 'except once when we were doing our regular change of shift DD drug check, one of the RNs made a comment about hoping we never needed anything for a weekend emergency. There isn't much choice for analgesics either.'

Ellena had been checking through the book. The IV phenobarb had not been the only drug returned to pharmacy by Linda, and suddenly she was angry with herself for not checking the supply of drugs long before this herself.

'I see that the supply of pethidine is lower than it should be also,' she said shortly. 'Mrs Richards still needs that at times. Please tell the afternoon staff I'll help check the drugs with them today, and sort a few things out.'

And then she groaned inwardly as she remembered Linda would be on duty and it would mean doing the check with her!

James Gill arrived only a few minutes later, the

occupational therapist and physiotherapist arrived together, and almost before Ellena knew it she was well into one of the most intensive, exhausting rounds she had ever done at Macallister's.

Chris Hansen was unfailingly kind and pleasant to the patients, but uncharacteristically terse with the medical staff, and after he had snapped at his DON a couple of times a tense atmosphere developed and there was none of the usual relaxed interchanges between the multi-discipline team. Then a couple of eyebrows were raised when the administrator joined them part-way through the round.

Chris nodded briefly at Ben, and then announced calmly, 'Mr Nicoletti asked if he could join us to gather some idea of the needs of the complex,' before turning to James Gill to ask him a question about Mr Harrington.

Ellena had tensed, and then called on all her years of training to ignore Ben's quiet presence in the background as they moved from patient to patient.

The nurses were kept busy bringing the patients to and from their rooms, always keeping a couple of rooms ahead. Once they slipped up, and it was Ellena who once again bore the brunt of the geriatrician's displeasure.

'If we're going to get through this round today, Miss Provis, it would help if the patients were ready,' he snarled as he rounded on her.

Suddenly Ellena had had enough of his sniping. 'I'm sorry, sir,' she said frostily, 'the nurses can't be expected to always anticipate when a patient will require changing or toileting. I'm sure it will only take us an extra minute to walk back to Mr Macgregor's room when he arrives. I do believe the patient's needs take priority over our time schedule.'

And then she grabbed the handles of the chart trolley, and pushed it forward so smartly that Ben had to move quickly out of the way to avoid being bumped into. She didn't see the twinkle in his eyes, nor the appreciative twitch of his moustache.

'The next patient is Mrs Brown,' Ellena said in a clear, no-nonsense voice as she stopped at the next door in the corridor. 'A left CVA six weeks ago. Managing on a pylon at home with daughter's assistance. I believe you saw her just before you went on leave, Dr Hansen, and admitted her for investigation of several unexplained falls and retraining in basic self-care skills. Dr Gill has changed her anti-hypertensive medication when regular testing proved she was experiencing postural hypotension contributing to her falls. Her blood-pressure is much more stable now.

'However,' she continued firmly as she thrust the chart at Chris, 'the nursing staff have reported several very brief lapses of consciousness this past week. At first Dr Gill thought she might have simply been dozing off. A sleep chart shows her sleep patterns. More than adequate sleep at night. As you will note, by her neurological chart observations I insisted the staff carry out, she does not respond to stimuli during those periods of only a few seconds. Appears to be TIAs. We believe another CAT scan could be desirable.'

No one moved a finger. No one seemed to breathe.

Nurses did not usually make such diagnostic statements. Not even DONs. Certainly not with such a proudly raised head, or such an aggressive tone of voice. Nor with such blazing eyes.

Dr Chris Hansen's expression was hidden as he read the chart in front of him. The only sound to break the silence was the rustle of the pages as he went through the chart.

'Oh, I remember now,' Ben suddenly said in a conversational tone, 'Mrs Brown's the old dear we helped pick up off the floor your first day back. That's right, isn't it, Ellena?'

Instead of relaxing the atmosphere, the tension increased as Ellena glared at him also.

'Well, you pushed the wheelchair closer for us, I believe, while Mrs Brown got herself up with floor drill, *Mr* Nicoletti!'

The bright smile on the handsome face never wavered at her sharp, sarcastic voice. 'And so fierce you were, protecting your patient from my inexperience, my dear love.'

This time his voice had deepened. It was warm and intimate. Reaching out to her. Setting her nerves tingling as she stared at him, not daring to believe the unbelievable. That light in his eyes for all to see was. . .it couldn't be. . .

Chris suddenly made a sound something between a snort and a choking sound. It brought her dazed eyes back to his face.

He was watching them with twinkling eyes. 'As she was protecting her patients a moment ago,' the consultant said in a rueful voice.

He still looked as though he was trying desperately not to laugh. And suddenly he was again the man Ellena had grown to think of as a close friend, no longer the angry, disagreeable doctor and employer.

'I'm very sorry, Ellena,' Chris said in a gentle voice, 'I've been very unfair and unreasonable.' Then he turned to the startled, puzzled trio near them. 'Look, Ben and I have something to sort out with our DON.

I'm sure you could all find something to do for the next hour.' Then he glanced at his watch. 'Or rather, what about an early lunch break, then you can catch up on some of your work until we're ready again?'

'And what about the patients already waiting in this next room, Dr Hansen?' James Gill said disapprovingly.

Chris was all consultant specialist again. 'You can check them and make my apologies for me, Dr Gill. We'll discuss them later,' he said calmly, and then slammed the chart in his hand back in the trolley.

He strode off down the corridor, leaving them all gaping after him.

That was, all except Ben. Ellena felt a firm hand grasp her elbow.

'After you, Ellena, sweetheart.'

Still in a daze, she turned her eyes from Chris's fast disappearing form back to the face so close to her own. He was smiling lovingly at her. This time there was definitely no mistaking that light in his face. Warm fingers slid to clasp her hand, and before she knew it, he was pulling her after him rapidly along the corridor.

Ben only paused briefly just past the nurses' station when a harried-looking nurse dashed towards them. 'Oh, Nurse White,' he called cheerfully, 'no more patients in their rooms until we let you know. Round postponed.'

'Ben! Ben, please. . .' Ellena gasped as she saw the startled expression on the EN's face as he pulled her past.

She gave her hand a tug. But he just tightened his grip.

Then he did stop. She felt him twirl her towards

him, and the soft feel of that luxurious moustache brushed her face, and warm, gentle lips kissed her. Then he was pulling her after him, and only then did she realise they had stopped fair smack in the centre of the lounge-room.

Ellena heard Lorraine's shocked voice say, 'Miss Provis!' And then the wheezy tones of old Sam Macgregor roared gleefully,

'Good on yer, mate. Give 'er another one!'

And then they were in her office, and the door slammed behind them.

Ben whirled her properly into his arms. His arms drew her right up against his body, and then he was still for a moment as he looked at her. She saw his dancing eyes coming closer, and shut her eyes.

'For goodness' sake, Ben! Can't that wait until we've sorted this other mess out?' said Chris's exasperated voice.

Ellena's head swivelled, and she saw with horror that Chris was standing behind them. She wrenched herself violently away from Ben.

'Now look what you've done, Chris Hansen,' Ben said mournfully.

'Ben Nicoletti! How. . .how dare you?'

He closed his eyes tightly. Then he opened them and shook his head. 'This woman says that far too much for my liking, Chris, old friend. What'll we do about it?'

Ellena was suddenly close to tears. Her throat closed up.

Ben's expression changed again just as Chris snapped, 'Behave yourself, Ben. Can't you see she's upset?'

But Ben had already reached up and brushed her

lips with the backs of his fingers. She flinched and he took a step back.

'Oh, sweetheart, I'm sorry. But you were so magnificent before, and I was so proud of you.' He rounded on Chris suddenly. 'You had no right to take it out on Ellena because you were so angry and upset.'

Ben was defending her. Her, Ellena Provis. Calling her sweetheart!

'I've already apologised for that,' Chris said stiffly. 'Please, let's sit down. We've got things to talk about.'

When they were seated he looked from one to the other, and then ran a hand through his thick hair.

'I told Ellena before what you said about speaking on the phone to her when she was on leave,' Ben said to him abruptly.

'But. . .' Ellena's voice still refused to function. She cleared her throat with an effort and tried again. 'I just don't understand, Chris. This morning is the first time I've spoken to you since the day. . .since. . .'

'Since you left here,' said Chris with a frown. 'Yes, I know. That's what Ben told me a while ago.'

Ellena flashed a look at the man beside her. He had believed her. A deep feeling of gratitude flowed up from that secret place in her that had once been so desperately hurt when only Gran had believed her when Howard, her husband, had told so many dreadful lies about her. Somehow the knowledge that the man she loved had faith in her calmed her. Strengthened her. Made her believe a little more that it had been love she had seen on his face. For her.

'Ben said it was the day Matthew collapsed,' she said quietly to Chris.

'Yes.'

'Did you ring my grandmother's home?'

'No, no,' Chris said impatiently. 'Matthew had told me you'd raced home because she was very ill. I rang the local hospital, of course.'

'And spoke to a Sister Provis,' Ben said softly.

She looked at him uncomprehendingly. And then shook her head. 'It definitely wasn't me you spoke to, then,' she said in a tight voice. 'It. . .it was the day of Gran's funeral. I no longer had a reason for being at the hospital.'

'But the woman I spoke to said her name was Provis! In fact agreed it was Ellena Provis.' Chris sounded bewildered. 'More than that, when I asked her if she could postpone her four weeks' annual leave and make do with the two weeks she'd already had off. . .' He paused, looking thoughtful. 'In fact, that was when she asked me if I was crazy, and. . .er. . .told me in no uncertain fashion what she thought of me.'

'But I never spoke to you!' insisted Ellena. 'Did you say who was speaking?'

'I'm not sure. Things were pretty much in a state here. I was very upset myself about not being with George and Jean.'

'And so some poor distant relation of Ellena's, called Provis, must have thought she had a lunatic on the phone wanting her to cancel her holidays!'

Chris and Ellena both looked at Ben. He spread out his hands and shrugged, watching Ellena, and then grinned triumphantly as comprehension dawned on her face.

'Of course! Irene Ellen, not Ellena Irene. It's a very old family name.'

'One of your few remaining relatives. A distant cousin, I think you said, last Friday?' Ben said softly.

Scalding heat filled her. There had been many other

things said last Friday. And done.

'Well, thank goodness that's one thing cleared up,' said Chris fervently. 'I'm very sorry, Ellena. I was all churned up about not being with my wife when George collapsed. They'd been staying with my parents in Sydney. All I could do at the time was leave this whole place in Ben's hands as soon as possible and take off.'

'Talk about letting me loose in a minefield!' Ben shook his head at his friend. 'There were the builders of the units with their workmen out on strike. Architects screaming in one ear. Suppliers who were having difficulties meeting deadlines. A head nurse no one liked. Trying to do payrolls from time-sheets not adequately checked.'

He suddenly smiled gently at Ellena as she started to protest. 'Oh, not after you came back, little love. Your meticulous work's been a tremendous relief.' He paused, and then added grimly, 'And then of course my biggest headache was Sister Linda Terry.'

'Yes, Linda Terry,' Chris said crisply. 'What you told me this morning about your suspicions and what that RN told you I've not had time to finish checking out yet.'

Ellena had been staring at Ben. No one had ever called her their 'little love' before. As Chris's words penetrated, she sat up straighter.

'What do you mean? What RN?' she asked sharply.

'The one who assured us Linda knew about the MRSA,' Ben said grimly. 'I rang her up, and then went to see her. Turned out she had a close friend who worked at one of the same hospitals Linda had for a brief period in Sydney. Sister Linda Terry's reputation had gone before her.'

'You should have told me, Ben,' Ellena began

sharply. 'Anything to do with my staff is my——'

'I know, I know,' he growled back at her, 'it was something you should have known. But, as the RN was very careful to point out, it was really only rumours and apparently there was no proof. And even then you. . .' This time he hesitated and shot a look at Chris. A dark tide of impatient anger swept into his face as he bit out at last, 'You had become very important to me, and she was so venomous towards you personally that I was afraid for you.'

Ellena was still staring at Ben in increasing wonder and delight when she heard his old friend murmur, 'Oh, how are the mighty fallen! Why didn't you appear on the scene years ago, Ellena? His friends and family have been trying to marry him off for years!'

This time it was Ellena's turn to blush scarlet as she saw Chris was openly laughing at them both. Then his amusement vanished. 'However, your plan to get Sister Terry to trust you didn't work, and we still have to think about what we're going to do about her,' he said heavily. 'Especially since you still haven't been able to come up with any proof, Ben.'

'Proof? Proof of what?'

The two men looked at each other, and it was Ben who answered her. 'Enough proof for her to never be able to legally practise again as a registered nurse,' Ben said harshly. He ignored Ellena's gasp of horror, and added quickly to Chris, 'and I still don't think we should tell Ellena. We'd have a better chance of catching Linda red-handed if we're right.'

'Now, just one moment——!'

'No, Ellena!' said Chris. 'I think Ben's right. Linda Terry is very clever. She managed to impress me greatly when I met her on Friday. And from what

Ben's already told me she has always been very careful never to have a witness even when she's been vicious to patients.'

'Vicious to patients!' Ellena exclaimed with horror.

'Mrs Davis told me a few things she had done to her. Oh, they happened before you came back, but she was only game to tell anyone after she found out you were back in charge for good,' Ben added rapidly as Ellena went pale. 'Our acting DON had told the old lady that no one would believe her. They would only think her mentally deficient. No RN with Linda's qualifications would ever call a patient the horrible names she had, or deliberately shower a patient in icy cold water when she threatened to report her.'

Ellena gasped speechlessly, and then a tide of fury swept through her. She sprang to her feet, but before she could find adequate words, Chris stood up also.

'That's only one of the reasons why this time it's so important there is absolute proof so that charges can be laid against her,' Chris said heavily before she could speak. 'And I have an idea, but I agree with you, Ben. Ellena will be able to play her part much better if she is unaware of what we believe is the RN's basic problem.'

Ellena opened her mouth to protest, but Ben rapped out, 'She's on afternoon shift today?' When Ellena nodded briefly, he continued, 'Right. If we can't put into practice what I'm thinking of today, I'm sure there'll be another time. Unfortunately,' he added almost to himself. 'Chris, I need to talk to you in your office.'

Chris stood up. 'We'll recommence the round of the patients at three this afternoon. And Ellena, I want you to make sure Sister Terry accompanies us. But whatever you do, don't let her know we've been discussing her at all. Just behave towards her as you always do.'

He turned to go, and paused as he thought of something else. 'I also expect you to know *exactly* what scheduled drugs you have in stock in future, Miss Provis,' he reprimanded her quite pleasantly, and added with a sudden glare, 'Please go and check through the DDs before rounds this afternoon! I want the stock brought up to the level we decided on when we opened. And I'd like to have a list in my hands by the time we recommence rounds of what we have in the cupboard at this moment. Is there anybody having regular painkillers at present?'

'Mrs Richards,' Ellena answered briefly, disliking intensely his criticism in front of Ben. Obviously he still didn't really have a clue how busy she'd been the last few weeks! 'Pethidine for pain in hip. Migrating screw in her pin and plate.'

'Right! Make sure there's still plenty of pethidine!'

Then he was gone, leaving Ellena looking after him with a startled frown. He was still annoyed with her for some reason.

Then suddenly the gentle touch of Ben's finger on the wrinkles of her forehead drove every thought away except the incredible knowledge that it was love for her she read in the expression on his face.

'Don't worry, my darling. We'll sort it out, and then. . .'

He heaved a deep sigh, and then she felt his lips touch hers. But even as she this time began to eagerly respond he wrenched himself away.

'No! This is still the wrong time, as you so rightly said a few days ago. But there's one thing I want you to know now. She followed me to church yesterday, and plonked herself beside me just before you arrived. I did *not* take her!'

'Ben!' called Chris, and then his grim face appeared around the corner. 'You can sort out your relationship with Ellena another time. Get in here!'

CHAPTER TWELVE

ELLENA didn't see Ben or Chris to speak to again until they strolled down the corridor towards the nurses' station at three o'clock. They were laughing together as they approached, and their cheerfulness was almost the last straw for Ellena.

The last few hours since their revelations about Linda had been the most frustrating of her life. She longed to know what they were keeping from her, but even more so, she had found it impossible to concentrate with everything still up in the air between herself and Ben.

One moment she was glowing with the certainty that he loved her. Then the next moment she was fighting her old demons and her lack of trust in men since a scoundrel called Howard had gone through a bigamous marriage ceremony with her in a desperate attempt to continue keeping her blind to his criminal activities.

The mirror in the staff-room at two-thirty had told her she looked pale and strained, but except for the slight frown that creased Ben's face as he glanced briefly at her, neither man paid her any attention.

There was a chorus of greetings for Dr Hansen from the staff that had just come on duty.

Chris beamed affably around at the group. 'Hello, everyone. It's good to be back. Now, all present for the round? Ah, Sister Terry, I do hope you're not too busy to accompany us this afternoon? I believe you held the fort for Miss Provis while she was sorting out her grandmother's estate.'

The answering beam on Linda Terry's face dimmed a little as she turned and raised her eyebrows at Ellena. 'Oh? Is *that* why you were away so long, Ellena? Why on earth did you let us all think you were simply on holiday?' she said reproachfully.

As though I had deliberately set out to keep it a secret, Ellena thought as she calmly answered the chorus of condolences.

'Perhaps we'd better get on with the round so Miss Provis can go off duty nearer time for a change?' Ben said at last quite firmly.

However, Chris seemed in no hurry, and except for her own tension that Ellena fought to control, he soon had them all relaxed. Except perhaps for James Gill, Ellena realised as Chris thoroughly examined Mrs Brown. She noticed that as Linda had gone to the other side of the bed to assist Chris with Mrs Brown's clothes, she had smiled intimately at James, but that he had quickly moved away from the woman's vicinity, a hunted look crossing his face.

A smile twitched Ellena's lips as she suddenly realised why the young doctor's rounds with Linda in the past had become so incomplete. He was running scared of the woman's advances!

She looked up to find Ben watching her with a knowing grin and sparkling eyes, which she suddenly found herself returning. Then she found she couldn't look away as his expression changed to one of blazing hunger and need.

'Miss Provis! Would you kindly pay attention?' Chris said with annoyance.

Her eyes flew to the geriatrician and she promptly dropped Mrs Brown's chart.

'I. . . I. . .' she stammered helplessly, and dived to retrieve it.

'Let Mr Nicoletti pick that up for you, seeing he continues to distract you,' Chris voice drawled.

There were a few stifled giggles, especially from the OT. Ellena could have sunk through the floor as Chris turned to Linda.

'Perhaps you could help me, Sister,' he said in an exasperated voice. 'Did you hear the question Miss Provis failed to?'

'Of course, sir,' she said loudly after turning around from glaring savagely at Ellena and Ben. 'The last episode of a supposed TIA was reported this morning just before lunch, the morning staff said. It appeared to last longer than other times. I believe if Miss Provis can find the neuro chart for you, it says a full minute.'

Chris frowned at her. 'Supposed? You don't think these lapses are transient ischaemic attacks, Sister Terry.'

'No, I don't,' Linda said confidently.

'Why?' asked Chris crisply. 'You've seen her actually having them yourself?'

Linda flushed slightly. 'As a matter of fact, no. I. . .'

'Then what do you base your assumption?' There was a decided chill in Chris relentless voice.

'It has been my experience that most old people drop off to sleep for a few moments during the day,' Linda said brightly, apparently unaware of the sudden stillness that had descended on the others.

There was silence for a moment as the consultant who was noted for his research into the sleep patterns of the aged stared thoughtfully at her.

'Really?' he said softly at last with a bite in his voice. 'And it has been my experience that very few geriatrics actually do so, and there is usually a reason for such lapses. Besides, someone merely asleep responds easily to stimuli, usually verbal as well as pain, Sister Terry.'

He turned away and explained to the worried Mrs Brown that he believed they should do a CAT scan, 'Just in case there's something going on in that old head of yours we should know about,' he finished gently.

Linda Terry had flushed awkwardly and remained silent. However, Chris continued to give her a hard time as the team proceeded from room to room.

They reached John Dredge at last who was pale and exhausted, with the oxygen still handy. He looked back at them calmly, his hands now only with their usual tremor. James Gill looked sharply at Chris who filled him in rapidly on what had happened that morning. Chris checked the old man over carefully with his stethoscope, listening intently to his heartbeat.

'You're fine, old friend,' he said cheerfully, 'just no more emotional upsets like that last one, please, or at least until we've sorted out your drug dosages.'

When they had left the room, Chris turned to Ben with a frown. 'Didn't you say his daughter-in-law upset him Friday morning?'

Ben nodded, and Chris swung around and glared at Linda. 'Were you aware of that, Sister?'

'Everyone in the place was,' Ben threw in drily. 'Mr Dredge's voice was very loud as he told Miss Burgess what he thought of her.'

'Then why isn't that reported in your nurse's report for the day, Sister Terry?'

'I. . .I. . .didn't think it was important enough,'

gasped the trembling RN as she saw the fury in Chris's face.

'It was a very stressful day for the staff, as you very well know, Dr Hansen,' Ellena suddenly said firmly.

No matter what Linda might or might not have done the DON was still ultimately responsible, and she'd never hesitated to stand up for her staff as she did now.

Chris stared back at her angrily, glared again at the white-faced, humiliated RN and then threw the chart back into the trolley and pulled out the next one.

It was Mrs Richards. Ellena noted that Linda was standing rigidly, holding herself with both hands across her waist as Chris moved the old lady's leg around carefully. He checked to see if there was any shortening of the leg that had been broken, and then asked Ellena to escort the old lady for a short walk so he could watch her progress in using the walking frame.

'Dr Hansen,' protested Ellena quickly, 'we're still waiting for the orthopaedic surgeon to see her, and Mrs Richards hasn't been allowed to weight-bear since her last X-ray. It's very painful for her.'

Chris drew himself up and stared haughtily at her.

'Then I suggest, Miss Provis, that we give her an analgesic now, and then I'll return to observe her progress when it has a chance to work. What have you prescribed for her, Dr Gill?'

Ellena stared in bewilderment at him. She'd already told him in the office about the pethidine, and his heartless request was so very unlike Chris that she opened her mouth to protest vigorously. She caught Ben's intent look, and slight shake of the head, and she stilled. It was James Gill who answered.

'Right,' Chris said sharply, 'Sister Terry, perhaps you'd like to organise that injection of pethidine, twenty-five milligrams, for Mrs Richards right away? We'll come back to her later.'

The still pale, agitated RN hurried away without a word.

Chris glanced at his watch and said softly, 'And I believe you said there was something you had to do about now, Ben?'

'Oh, yes,' said Ben sharply, 'and I need Miss Provis to help me.'

Before she could protest, Chris nodded. 'But take your time, won't you? It should take a couple of minutes or so.'

As he turned away, he suddenly looked very grim. Ben grabbed Ellena firmly by the elbow and started ushering her away.

'Ben, what on earth are you doing?' she hissed breathlessly as they got out of earshot.

'You'll see. I hope,' he added sharply.

He paused as they neared the treatment-room. 'You always have to get another nurse to check pethidine, right?' he whispered.

She stared at him in bewilderment. He laid a finger across his lips.

'Yes,' she snapped softly, 'but she can get Joan Wheat to——'

'But not to actually watch her draw it up?'

'She should,' Ellena snapped, 'but sometimes when we are all very busy, all nurses are guilty of drawing up the——' She stopped, and then continued very softly in dawning realisation, 'Drawing up the pethidine by themselves, and we only check the empty ampoule to make sure they have the right drug.'

Ben moved silently and peered in the glass porthole set in the closed door of the treatment-room.

'Uh-oh, bingo!' he hissed exultantly after a moment, and then thrust the door wide open, dragging Ellena in with him.

Linda froze in the act of pushing the plunger of the syringe. The needle was in the top of her own outer arm, deep in the muscle where pethidine injections had to be given.

'Sister Terry!' gasped Ellena faintly, shocked to her depths.

She moved forward and picked up a small, empty glass container. Next to it was an opened ampoule of sterile water.

'So that's how you've been getting away with it,' said Ben furiously. 'You get the real stuff to stop your cravings and a poor old lady in severe pain gets water! Get Chris, Ellena. Tell him it's worked.'

Everything after that remained a haze for Ellena for some time. She was aware that Linda had still just stood there white and trembling when she had returned from ringing the police as instructed grimly by Chris. Then the shocked woman had been whipped away to Ben's office to eventually be escorted away by the police. But her blank, lifeless eyes and her haggard face were to haunt Ellena for a long time afterwards.

'I found out after ringing a close friend of mine, a deputy DON at the hospital in Sydney Ben's informant told us about, that she'd had a back injury just over two years ago,' Chris told Ben and Ellena later. 'They'd suspected her of drug addiction. Too many analgesics prescribed for pain, the poor devil. Pethidine and other drugs had gone missing, but they hadn't been able to definitely trace it to her. She went from being one of their best nurses to a very unreliable and bitter one whom nobody liked working with. They'd just been mightily relieved when she had resigned. Must have thought all her Christmases had come at once when she arrived here and suddenly found herself acting DON! And then she had some crazy idea that by discrediting Ellena she might even get the job permanently.'

'Oh, the poor woman,' Ellena murmured with tears springing to her eyes, 'how dreadfully she must have hated herself!'

There was a stunned silence for a moment.

Then Chris exclaimed furiously, 'The poor woman! Think of the poor patients she left in pain.'

'Oh, I am,' cried Ellena, 'but that's just the point! She must have been in a dreadful mental and physical turmoil to do that to her patients. She was an excellent nurse once by those glowing references in her folder! And all because of a back injury!'

The men just stared helplessly at her as the tears started to flow down her cheeks.

'Ellie. . .' Ben began in a strangled voice.

'And what have you done to upset her now?' a new voice cried as there was a flurry of skirts and Ellena felt soft arms go around her.

'Jean, what are you doing here?' Chris said in an exasperated voice. 'I thought I told you. . .'

'I know what you told me,' his beautiful young wife tossed over her shoulder, 'but I saw the police drive off, and I just couldn't wait any longer. I guessed how upset poor Ellena would be.'

'And don't you think Ben is just dying to comfort her, too?' her husband said with mock sternness.

'Oh, of course you are, Ben, dear!' Jean beamed at their exasperated friend as she stood up. She looked back at Ellena, who was staring from one to the other.

'Oh, I do wish I'd thought to introduce you two ages ago. You're just right for each other,' she added enthusiastically.

'I'm quite capable of recognising that for myself,' growled Ben suddenly, 'but we haven't had a chance even to discuss our relationship yet!'

'Then it's about time you did,' said Chris with mock solemnity, but still decisively. 'The Macallister Rehabilitation Complex can no longer tolerate such carryings on between its administrator and DON as was seen by patients and staff alike today! You're both off duty as of now! Oh, and this is yours, I believe, Ellena,' he added as he dropped her crumpled resignation on to the desk, 'I certainly don't want it! It just put me in a vile mood!'

He grabbed hold of his laughing wife and started hauling her towards the door. But Jean hung back for a moment and said mischievously, 'And if you want me to be the matron of honour at your wedding, *please* make the wedding date no later than two months' time or I'll be too obviously pregnant!'

'Jean!' uttered the father-to-be speechlessly.

Then they had disappeared, their voices echoing back down the corridor, leaving Ben and Ellena staring helplessly at each other across the width of the room.

'Shall we, Ellena?' Ben said at last in a voice suddenly very uncertain.

'Shall we what?' she answered faintly.

His fingers smoothed down his moustache fast. Her head drooped as she followed the action with her eyes. He took a step towards her, and then paused and looked around him with frustration.

'Why have so many of our encounters been in this blessed office?' he muttered.

She stood up shakily and moved over to the window.

'Not all of them,' she said in a low voice, and lifted a trembling hand out to touch an African violet. Gran was suddenly very close.

Then she felt his hands gently hold her shoulders and turn her around to face him. A whole charge of high-voltage electricity began to sweep through her at the burning look of love in his face.

'Shall we get married? And soon?'

She stared at him unbelievingly.

'I think I've loved you from that very first evening,' he murmured huskily. 'By the time I'd worked beside you for a couple of days, I knew for certain. But then. . .'

'But then?' she managed to croak.

'Then I realised Linda was out to get you the sack so she could get your position. She even applied for the deputy's job as I knew she would,' he said savagely.

'That MRSA business,' said Ellena slowly.

He nodded. 'And when that failed there would have been other attempts, but it was that and her almost pathological hatred of you that scared me.'

'Enough to be horrible to me when she was around!' Ellena flashed. 'And when I saw you sitting with her in church. . .'

'Oh, my darling,' he said harshly, and she saw the remembered pain twist his face. 'She'd just sat beside me, and I was at first merely annoyed with her. Then I saw you walk in. I had to sit through that whole service watching your lovely face, wishing desperately it were you beside me, knowing what you would think when you saw me with her. By then I knew she was irrational, even more dangerous than I had suspected, and I dared not antagonise her further until Chris got

back. You can't imagine the relief I felt this morning
to see him at last!

'I'd even gone down to that Sydney hospital to make
some enquiries about her, but of course it was
Saturday, and no one on duty that I spoke to
remembered her. Or so they said,' he added with a
rueful smile. 'You medical people stick together, don't
you? It only took Chris one phone call! Thank God
it's all over.'

He suddenly groaned, and put his arms tightly
around her. She gave a deep, blissful sigh and melted
against him. They just held each other for a moment,
and then Ben stirred and she lifted her face for his kiss.

He started to bend towards her and then checked,
'Do you really want us to stay here,' he whispered,
'or shall we go somewhere else?'

She stilled. Then she pulled away and suddenly
grinned at the scowl that darkened his face. She felt
as though she danced on wings as she raced across to
the door, turned the lock and switched off the
main light.

He also had a smile from ear to ear as she turned
back. His hand finished taking the phone off the hook.

'I think this is the biggest nuisance,' he murmured
as she arrived back in front of him.

He reached out for her again, and then stopped as
she suddenly thought of something and froze.

'What is it?' he asked in concern.

'Ben, there's something in my past that you don't
know about yet.'

He looked suddenly self-conscious. 'I don't think so,
my lovely girl. Especially if you're referring to Howard.
I know all about that rotten sod,' he said rapidly.
'Don't look like that, my poor sweetheart,' he added

fiercely, and suddenly hauled her back into his arms.

But she remained stiff and unresponsive. 'You know about the. . .the bigamous marriage?' she said hesitantly.

'And about the lies he told about your knowing all about his illegal drug dealings. And about the jury's verdict of innocent at your trial as an accessory. Chris told me not long after he first employed you.'

'Chris knows too?' she said in a dazed voice.

'Believe me, he checked thoroughly on the person he thought the best candidate for his DON position! And we all admire you tremendously for the way you pulled your life together. You've more than proved yourself since you've been here, my darling. Chris told me that a long time ago. Before we ever met. The first time he ever had any doubt about you was when he rang you at Scone.'

He paused, and she felt a tremor pass through him.

'And now,' he pleaded in an unsteady voice, 'you haven't told me you love me yet, and that you'll marry me as soon as possible?'

Suddenly Ellena felt wonderfully, gloriously alive. She lifted her face up to his, and he drew in a sharp breath at the brilliance of it.

'We certainly can't disappoint that cheeky mother-to-be, can we,' she said solemnly, despite her laughing eyes, 'or old Sam Macgregor who ordered you to give me another kiss? Besides, this matron loves you quite desperately and absolutely insists——' She gasped as his devouring lips cut off her imperious words.

And then there was only the taste of him, the touch of his arms as they strained together. And as before, it wasn't enough. She needed him to touch every inch of her. She needed to belong to him body and soul.

Ben's fingers were on the buttons of her blouse, when he stopped. 'It's no good,' he groaned indistinctly, 'I keep waiting to hear a knock on the door. Let's get out of here!'

A few moments later, Ellena's laughing protests rang out across the car park, as they ran hand in hand to the car.

A flutter of movement in the garden next door caught her eye. She glanced across and saw Chris and Jean watching them, with their arms around each other. They both waved, just as Ben swung Ellena around and kissed her thoroughly.

Then she was in the car, and as it pulled out of the car park, she went to wave to them, but they were engrossed in each other. Chris's hand was resting on the gentle swell of his wife's abdomen, and as she watched, he pulled her into his arms.

Ellena sighed happily and looked across at Ben. It was all going to be just perfect.

'Ben, you will stay on as administrator?' she asked suddenly.

He glanced across at her with a raised eyebrow. 'Of course. At least, as long as I and the DON can work out our various roles a bit better,' he teased her.

Ellena's heart swelled as she smiled tremulously back at him. She would be working beside him, helping to bring to complete fruition the Hansens' dream of ongoing care for many old people.

'It couldn't be more perfect,' she said out loud in a dreamy voice.

'Oh, yes, it could!' exclaimed Ben. His hand reached out and clasped hers. 'We aren't married yet!'

And as she clung to him, she knew he was right. It was just going to get better. . .and better.

Full of Eastern Passion...

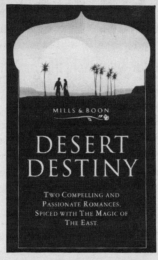

Savour the romance of the East this summer with
our two full-length compelling Romances,
wrapped together in one exciting volume.

AVAILABLE FROM 29 JULY 1994   PRICED £3.99

MILLS & BOON

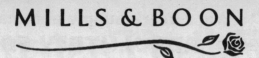

Win a Year's Supply of romances
ABSOLUTELY FREE!

YES! you could win a whole year's supply of Mills & Boon romances by playing the Treasure Trail Game. Its simple! - there are seven separate items of treasure hidden on the island, follow the instructions for each and when you arrive at the final square, work out their grid positions, (i.e **D4**) and fill in the grid reference boxes.

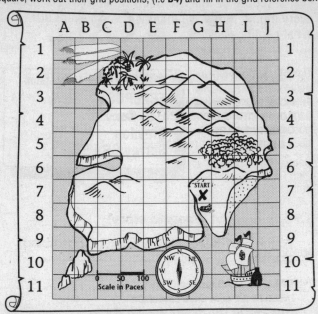

From the start, walk 250 paces to the **North**.

GRID REFERENCE

From this position walk 150 paces **South**.

GRID REFERENCE

Then 100 **South**.

GRID REFERENCE

Now turn **West** and walk 150 paces.

GRID REFERENCE

Now take 100 paces **East**.

GRID REFERENCE

And finally 50 paces **East**.

GRID REFERENCE

Please turn over for entry details

SEND YOUR ENTRY
NOW!

The first five correct entries picked out of the bag after the closing date will each win one year's supply of Mills & Boon romances (six books every month for twelve months - worth over £90). What could be easier?

Don't forget to enter your name and address in the space below then put this page in an envelope and post it today (you don't need a stamp).

Competition closes 28th Feb '95.

TREASURE TRAIL Competition
FREEPOST
P.O. Box 236
Croydon
Surrey CR9 9EL

Are you a Reader Service subscriber?   Yes ☐   No ☐

Ms/Mrs/Miss/Mr _____ COMTT

Address _____

_____

_____

Postcode _____

Signature _____

One application per household. Offer valid only in U.K. and Eire. You may be mailed with offers from other reputable companies as a result of this application. Please tick box if you would prefer not to receive such offers. ☐